AUG 18 1970 6/85 ⑦

W9-CPK-343

C.1

J
HOD

Hodges, Margaret
  The freewheeling of Joshua Cobb. Illus
by Richard Cuffari. Farrar, Straus &
Giroux [c1974]
108p illus

A carefree bicycle trip to New England
brings trouble to young Joshua

NAPA CITY-COUNTY LIBRARY
1150 Division St.
Napa, California 94558

1 Bicycles and bicycling--Fiction 2 Camp-
ing--Fiction I Illus II T

00466   TI   614932   ©THE BAKER & TAYLOR CO.   5083

The Freewheeling of Joshua Cobb

by MARGARET HODGES

One Little Drum
What's for Lunch, Charley?
A Club Against Keats
Tell It Again: Great Tales
from Around the World (*editor*)
The Secret in the Woods
The Wave
The Hatching of Joshua Cobb
Constellation (*editor*)
Sing Out, Charley!
Lady Queen Anne
The Making of Joshua Cobb
Hopkins of the Mayflower
The Other World
The Freewheeling of Joshua Cobb

The Freewheeling

MARGARET HODGES

of Joshua Cobb ✸ ✸ ✸

ILLUSTRATED BY
RICHARD CUFFARI

FARRAR, STRAUS AND GIROUX ✸ NEW YORK

DISCARD

NAPA CITY-COUNTY LIBRARY
1150 Division St.
Napa, California 94558

Copyright © 1974 by Margaret Hodges
All rights reserved
First printing, 1974
Printed in the United States of America
Published simultaneously in Canada by
Doubleday Canada Ltd., Toronto

Designed by Millicent Fairhurst

Acknowledgment is made with thanks to the Co-
operative Recreation Service, Inc., Delaware, Ohio, for
permission to quote "Canoe Round," from *101 Rounds*.

LIBRARY OF CONGRESS CATALOGING IN PUBLICATION DATA

Hodges, Margaret.
  The freewheeling of Joshua Cobb.

  [1. Bicycles and bicycling—Fiction. 2. Camping—
Fiction] I. Cuffari, Richard, illus. II. Title.
PZ7.H664Fr [Fic] 74-11456
ISBN 0-374-32464-6

This book is for
all hands
on the great trip,
June 1973,

Gaffer

Fletch

Chantal

Cordie

Rebecca

Art

Eloise

Arthur

Susanna

Alex

Johnny

Ingola*

from
Grumma

* and Sven too

The Freewheeling of Joshua Cobb

1 ❀ ❀

All that summer the roads were full of bicycles. As early as June, Joshua Cobb and Dusty Moore saw them on every road when Dusty was driving Josh home from boarding school.

On the small back roads, bicycle riders panted uphill and coasted downhill, crouched over their handlebars. Some traveled light, carrying nothing much except a change of clothes in a wire basket. Some carried every sort of equipment, sleeping bags, plastic tents, little stoves, pots and pans, everything but the kitchen sink.

Even on the big main roads where no cyclists dared

to go, the bicycles were there, lashed to the front or rear of vans and campers and trucks. Often the bicycles rode upside down on the tops of cars, tied to special racks. All were speeding toward the back roads where cyclists could ride in comparative safety.

"And that's what I want to do," said Dusty. "I've saved my pay from the Marine Corps and my leave is extended to thirty days, plus travel time, because I'm changing duty stations. I've got a job lined up on a farm for a couple of weeks. Then I want to take a bicycle trip, not a long one, just New England for about ten days. Want to come?"

Want to! It knocked the wind out of him to think of it—a bicycle trip with Dusty, his favorite counselor at camp last summer, his good friend ever since. Dusty had no family of his own, but he was a welcome visitor to Josh and his mother, and called them his "family." Josh's father was dead and he had no brother, but Dusty was like a brother or a father. Better, maybe, if you could believe what some of the guys at Oakley School said about their brothers and fathers. Dusty was the best male Josh had met so far, and so far he was interested mostly in males, except for his mother and one other person.

"Have you got a bike?" Dusty asked. "You need a fairly good one for a trip."

"It's fairly good," Josh said. "It's got three gears."

"That's enough," said Dusty. "Have you still got your sleeping bag from camp?"

Josh still had his sleeping bag. "But what about money?" he asked. "How much would the trip cost?"

"Not much if we get enough people and share expenses. There's a girl I know—her family owns the farm where I'm going to work—and she wants to try camping. She thinks we could use one of the farm trucks. Name's Muff. Muff Bacon. Can you get some other people your age?"

Josh hesitated, then asked, "Male or female?"

"Doesn't matter, as long as they're in shape to go forty miles a day," Dusty said. "I'll get some letters from people who know me—from camp, and the Marines, and maybe your mother would write one— so your friends will know I'm O.K. Tell them we'll start from the Gitche Gumee Campground—that's near Rivertown—and we'll end the trip there, too."

When they explained it to Mrs. Cobb, she said, "Of course I'll write a letter of recommendation for you, Dusty. I have complete confidence in you." Then, just as Dusty and Josh were relaxing, sure that the trip was on, she asked Dusty, "Have you ever taken this trip before?"

He had not.

"There won't be a single person all along the way whom you know and can depend on? You can't control everything. What about accidents, and sickness?"

"I'm a member of American Youth Hostels," Dusty told her. "We'll use hostels. They would help."

"Yes, but—" said Mrs. Cobb. She looked more and more doubtful, and brought up more and more reasons for saying no to the bicycle trip.

Josh had thought all along that the trip was too good to be true. Even so, before he fell asleep that night, he thought about who might have gone with him. He no longer had the addresses of guys from Camp Buddy. His closest friends now were the ones he had made at Oakley School. His roommate wouldn't have been a good bet. He was hard to please and had to have everything exactly right. And Josh wouldn't have asked Brillo Brilovich, even though he was fun. Brillo wasn't athletic enough to bicycle forty miles a day. G. G. Graham would have been the best. G.G. lived in New York, not too far away, but money would be a problem for him. On the other hand, G.G. was used to solving problems, and he was in good shape. He had stroked the crew on which Josh had rowed that spring at Oakley School.

There was one other person Josh would have liked to ask. Helen Crane. Her brother had been the head prefect at Oakley. Helen went to school near Oakley, and Josh had thought a lot about her from the moment when he had bumped into her, skating on the river last winter. He still remembered the way she had looked, skimming over the ice in a red cap and red jacket. He remembered the way she had looked every time he had seen her. Sometimes he dreamed about Helen.

He'd see her again in the fall, and she had said, "You could write to me." She had also promised him a dance, the first time there was one at school. But fall was a long way off. What if she could have come with him on the bicycle trip? When he fell asleep, he dreamed that Helen was bicycling beside him, wearing a red jacket. It would have been great, but it had been too good to be true. When his mother said no, she meant no.

Then, in the morning, just as Dusty was getting ready to leave for his farm job, Mrs. Cobb suddenly said, "Josh, I hardly slept a wink last night, thinking about that bicycle trip. I can't bear to keep you in town and make you miss such an adventure. Let's talk about it some more."

So they talked about it some more, and at last she said, "I'll worry every minute, but if you'll help to earn the money, you can go."

Josh was flabbergasted, and Dusty was triumphant. "Don't you worry, Mrs. Cobb," he said. "One of the best things about hosteling is that everybody takes care of everybody else. And American Youth Hostels has a complete set of rules for safety. We'll follow them absolutely." The last thing he said to Josh was, "When you get some more people for the trip, let me know."

There were still some hurdles ahead, but the impossible trip was now possible. Josh lost no time in writing to G. G. Graham. It took more nerve to write to Helen. How could he explain the whole idea of the trip so that she'd want to say yes and her parents wouldn't say no?

He rewrote that letter several times and finally added a note he thought might help:

P.S. There'll be another girl, Muff Bacon. Actually, she is not a girl. She's as old as Dusty, around twenty, and she will take care of you. I hope you can go.

He had almost written, "I will take care of you," but decided not to say that. Oh sure, if a friend broke his arm, Josh would stick with him. He had done that at Camp Buddy. If a dog, even a dog he didn't like, was about to drown, Josh would get him out of the water. He had done that at Oakley School. But inside himself Josh knew that he was not too well co-ordinated, not too well organized. He couldn't guarantee to take care of anyone else. He had enough trouble taking care of himself.

In the next few weeks, Josh took on every job he could find, cutting grass, washing cars, baby-sitting.

In between jobs he waited to hear from G.G. and Helen, but no letters came.

Then one evening, out of the blue, Helen's mother telephoned, and Josh's mother talked to her. Josh, hovering nearby, knew from the way his mother sounded that all was going well. "I know . . . I know . . . These days you hear of teenagers traveling across the country together and they don't even know each other's last names! But I must say, this trip is well planned and fairly sane."

When Mrs. Cobb hung up, she said, "It's all right. Helen can go on the bicycle trip. Her sister, Cassandra, will come too."

Josh couldn't believe his luck. It was no dream. It was really going to happen. And if Helen's sister was anything like her, it would be twice as good. G.G. would make six, if he could come, and Dusty wrote that that would be a good number. Six people sharing expenses would make it easy. He sent a booklet about bicycle trips, and Josh collected the things he should take: his sleeping bag, a tire-repair kit, a tin plate and cup, a fork, a spoon, and a knife, a screwdriver and a monkey wrench, a flashlight and a canteen for water, sunglasses, swimming trunks and a towel, soap and a comb, a change of clothes, a raincoat, a sweater, and of course a toothbrush.

"I'll send a check to Dusty for your part of the expenses," his mother said. "The money you earn can be for emergencies. You should have some cash with you in case of trouble, and you should carry it in a money belt, for safety."

"I'll get one," Josh said. "Don't worry."

Luckily, his bicycle was in good shape. He used it delivering papers and going to and from his other jobs. At least he wasn't getting soft before this trip started. But why didn't G.G. write?

It was ten days before G.G.'s letter came, post-marked not from New York but from Oakley School.

Dear Josh,

I can go! My folks think the trip sounds great. I'll bet you're surprised I'm at school. I went home, but there was nothing to do, so I came back to work with some guys on the school farm. Swing Lowe is here and some other teachers too. I asked the other guys, but none of them can go on the trip. Swing says I can borrow his bike. We can put it on his car and he'll drive me to where the trip starts. I can pay expenses with what I earn here, plus some money from home. See you. Take it easy.

G.G.

On the last day, Josh loaded his bike. He would take the train from home to Rivertown. His bike would travel in a baggage car. At Rivertown, Josh would begin to bicycle, riding alone to Gitche Gumee Campground; it was only about ten miles. No problem. He had fastened his sleeping bag on the rear luggage carrier and was packing the front basket when the mailman arrived. There was a letter for Josh. He had had a letter with writing like that at school, and he knew right away that it was from Helen.

Dear Josh [she wrote],

The worst thing has happened. I have to have my tonsils out and I can't come on the bicycle trip. I just found out or I would have told you sooner. Imagine how I feel. Instead of bicycling around New England and having a wonderful time, I'll be sitting here with a sore throat, doing nothing. But my sister, Cassandra, is coming, even if I can't. She's shy, so I hope you'll take care of her. I really feel terrible, and not just about my throat. Have a good time anyway.

Sincerely,
Helen

P.S. Cassandra hates her name. She likes to be called Crane.

11

2 ❀ ❀

It was a big disappointment, the biggest Josh had ever had. If Helen couldn't come, he would rather have no girls at all. But the excitement of leaving home was big too.

His mother was full of advice. "Don't talk to strangers, at least not until you get together with your group. And no matter what happens, don't hitchhike. Send me a postcard now and then, and call me collect from anywhere if you get into real trouble."

Even while she waved goodbye to him at the railroad station, she thought of one more worry. "Oh, Josh, you forgot to buy that money belt. Watch out for your wallet."

On the train, Josh read and reread his hosteling handbook, memorizing the rules. Two hours later, as the baggage master handed down the bicycle from the baggage car at Rivertown, he remembered to check his wallet. His name and address were there. So was Dusty's last letter, telling where they would stay every night on the trip. So was Josh's emergency fund, twenty-five dollars, his own earnings. All O.K., stashed away in his back pocket.

He checked over his bike. His sleeping bag was firmly tied to the rear, and the front basket was evenly balanced. Josh shifted his knapsack to a comfortable spot between his shoulders, swung onto the saddle, and pedaled away from the Rivertown railroad station. This was it, really the start of the trip. For the first time in his life, he was alone on the open road. Nobody who knew him knew exactly where he was. He didn't know exactly, either.

He stopped at a gas station to get a map and ask the way to the Gitche Gumee Campground. That didn't count as "talking to strangers."

"You can't miss it," said the man at the gas pump. "Follow Main Street to River Road and turn right. Gitche Gumee is about ten miles. But look out. Traffic's pretty heavy in town."

Josh pedaled into Main Street, keeping to the right-hand side of the road and riding in a straight line, with the traffic. He obeyed the traffic signals and stop signs, but even so, several cars honked at him and he thought he might be squashed like a bug between the cars. Once, when he pulled up behind a truck, the driver gunned his engine, letting a blast of hot fumes escape from his exhaust into Josh's face.

He was glad when he came to the end of the crowded shopping district on Main Street and turned into River Road. Before long, he was passing wide green lawns under shady trees. He began to relax and felt safe enough to take his eyes off the road.

Feeling safe was a mistake. Just ahead was a driveway where a car stood, its motor idling. Suddenly the car backed into the road, and Josh crashed into it. He heard the crunch of metal against metal and felt a jolt that threw him from his bicycle. For a moment everything turned black. Then he found himself lying in the gutter with his bike on top of him. As he brought his eyes into focus, the car window opened and the angry red face of a woman glared down at him.

"Why don't you watch where you're going? Look what you've done to my car!" she said in a voice trembling with rage.

Josh picked himself up from the gutter and sat down on the curb, feeling dizzy, as if his brains had been jerked loose. He looked at his bike. He didn't know yet whether he was really hurt, but his bike certainly was. The front fender was bent at a terrible angle. He looked up at the woman. "But you—you—" he said.

She got out of the car and ran into the house at the far end of the driveway. Josh could hear her shrill voice in the house, and he heard the loud, heavy voice of a man answering her. Then he stood up, walked along the driveway to the house, and looked in through the open door. The woman was there, arguing with a man. He too looked angry.

When he saw Josh, he said, "What do you want?"

"She backed into me," Josh said in a shaky voice.

"Who says so?" the man asked. "Where's your witness?"

"She is," Josh said, looking at the woman.

The man gave a short laugh. "*She* is? Get out of here before we sue you for scratching our car!"

Josh was shaken. Witness! Sue! He almost ran back to his bike and started pushing it along the road. The front fender scraped the tire at every turn of the wheels, and the back fender was wobbly. Josh himself was wobbly. What should he do? Should he call his mother? She had said to call her if he got into real trouble. But she was worried already. She'd worry even more if he told her what had happened. He was afraid to argue with that man and woman any more. He sat down on the curb again to think about it.

Dusty always said, "Keep loose." Josh decided to keep loose now, if he could. He looked at his bike again and remembered the screwdriver and monkey wrench. Fishing into his basket, he found them and set to work with shaking fingers. He tightened the back fender, but the front one looked like a snake, and he soon found that to get the fender off, he'd have to take off the front wheel too. Maybe there was a repair shop in Rivertown where he could have it really fixed. Yes, the bicycle handbook listed Buzz's Bicycle Shop in the center of Rivertown.

It seemed twice as far, pushing his bike back into town, but at last he found Buzz's Bicycle Shop. It was on a side street, and Buzz himself was there, tinkering with a tangle of bicycles. He was a slow-moving man.

Josh explained his trouble and Buzz was sympathetic. "Tough luck," he said. "But maybe I can fix your fender. I might get to it some time tomorrow."

"Tomorrow!" Josh said. "I've got to get to Gitche Gumee Campground today, or it'll mess up a whole trip for four other people."

Buzz looked at Josh's stricken face. "Oh well," he said, "I guess I can look at it now." When he had looked at it, he told Josh, "It'll be three dollars."

"That's O.K.," Josh said, and reached for his back pocket. It was empty. But it couldn't be! He felt again. Nothing. He searched all his other pockets. Zilch! His wallet was definitely gone.

"My money's gone," he said hopelessly. "Everything I earned. My wallet must have dropped out of my pocket when I fell."

"Wow!" Buzz said. "This sure is your unlucky day. Must be some sort of a jinx. Anyone loses a wallet these days, that money's gone. G-O-N-E, gone. But take it easy. I'll fix you up some way. Don't panic. Things usually work out."

"I can't pay," Josh began.

"Forget it." Buzz took a big pizza out of a paper bag and said, "Have some."

"Thanks a lot," Josh said. He ate a slice of pizza, chewing fast, as if that would hurry things along, and waited while Buzz slowly finished the rest of the pizza and slowly went back to work. An hour went by. Two hours. At last Buzz began tinkering with Josh's bike. He removed the front wheel and looked again at the fender.

"Listen," he said, "I can't fix this thing, and you don't really need a fender. I'll just put your wheel back on and you won't owe me anything."

"Thanks a lot," Josh said again. "I really mean it."

Evening traffic was filling the streets of Rivertown by the time he steered his bike to the curb and mounted the saddle.

"You'll be all right when you get to your friends at Gitche Gumee," Buzz said.

"I guess so," Josh called back, "if that jinx isn't still on me."

As he pulled away, he heard Buzz advising, "You should tell the police about your wallet. Not much chance you'll get it back, but you should do that."

Josh decided not to tell the police. Both his watch and his stomach told him it was getting late. His stomach felt worse than empty. It felt nervous. What if Dusty and the others couldn't wait and he never caught up with them? He saw himself wobbling along strange roads, on and on, living on an occasional pizza. Anyway, as Buzz had said, Josh would probably never see his wallet again. He'd better push on to Gitche Gumee Campground.

Keeping close to the curb, Josh made his way out of the Rivertown traffic. When he passed the scene of his accident, he slowed down enough so that he could see his wallet if it was there in the gutter where he had fallen. This was the most likely place to have dropped it. If not, it was hopeless anyway. But it was not in the gutter. Not in the road anywhere around. It was gone all right. G-O-N-E, gone.

About nine long miles ahead lay Gitche Gumee, and the road was beginning to climb. Suddenly Josh felt all in. He had eaten only a few bites of pizza since he had left home. He wondered if he could pedal nine miles, or even climb one hill. Buzz at the bicycle shop had said, "Don't panic. Things usually work out." But how were they going to work out now? He got off his bike and sat down by the side of the road.

At that moment, a car passed him, stopped, and backed up. A bicycle was riding on the rear rack, and inside the car were Swing Lowe and G. G. Graham.

"Cobb!" G.G. shouted in greeting.

Mr. Lowe leaned over, looked down at Josh, and said in his usual calm, schoolmasterish way, "Well, Cobb, what are you doing here?"

It was like a miracle. Help had come.

"Sir, I'm trying to get to Gitche Gumee Campground," said Josh.

"You won't get anywhere sitting down," Swing said. "Hop in. Graham, give me a hand with Cobb's bike. Luckily, the rack will hold two."

The road was short and easy now, and Josh felt like a new man as he told all his troubles, ending with, "I'm sure glad you saw me."

G.G. grinned. "You showed up like a berry in a bowl of milk."

At the wheel of the car Swing Lowe said, "H'm, h'm," in a sympathetic way. "But you should have reported your accident to the police. I'll do it for you, and leave your name and address at that house on my way back, if you'll tell me where it is. I doubt that those people will follow it up. I think the woman felt she was to blame and they panicked."

"She was a bum and he was a bum and it was a bum deal," G.G. said flatly.

Ahead, they saw a sign reading GITCHE GUMEE CAMPGROUND. Swing Lowe pulled his car to a stop where a dirt road turned off into a grove of tall pine trees.

"Here you are," he said. "Let's hope your troubles are all behind you. But in case you haven't got the hex sign off you yet, I happen to have ten dollars to spare. Take it as a loan, for emergencies."

He wouldn't listen to thanks. Good old Swing! A friend in need, no doubt about it. Josh stashed away Swing's ten dollars in a shirt pocket that buttoned down. Then he and G.G. lifted their bikes from the rack, and Josh saw that G.G.'s, the one Swing Lowe had loaned him, was a ten-speed bike. They watched him drive off with a final wave. Now to find Dusty, thought Josh, and Muff, and—not Helen, but her sister anyway. Maybe the girls would be O.K. after all.

Slowly, Josh and G.G. pedaled through the campground. The air was cool, and there was a good smell of wood smoke and of food. In clearings through the woods, small fires blazed cheerfully, and quiet groups of campers were cooking, eating, or resting. Each group had its car, or truck, or trailer, some almost as big as houses. Tents of all sizes made bright spots of color in the late-afternoon sunlight.

"But where is our bunch?" G.G. wondered. "What if they aren't here?"

"Don't panic," Josh advised. And just then a familiar voice called, "Looking for someone?"

There was Dusty in a clearing at the far end of the campground. Two girls were standing beside him, one short, one tall. The tall one must be Muff, thought Josh. The short one would be Helen's sister, the one he was to take care of. Behind them stood an old farm truck, battered and long unpainted, except for some straggly letters on its side: I, A TRUCK, AM DOING THE BEST I CAN.

Josh pedaled full speed ahead and G.G. followed suit. They swung off their bikes and parked them beside two others that stood near the truck. Ten-speed bikes, Josh noted. He was the only one with just three speeds.

Dusty loped forward to meet them. "Thought you'd never get here," he said, in the warm, easygoing way that Josh liked. "We were ready to ride and spread the alarm." He took off his old Marine fatigue cap and held out his hand, looking at G.G. "You're

Graham, I guess. Come on, you and Josh. Meet the girls.''

He nodded at the short girl. "This is Muff Bacon.''

The first thing Josh noticed about Muff's face was that she had a scar on her chin. The rest of her face was mostly hidden behind a pair of big dark goggles. Not wanting to stare at the scar, Josh looked down. Muff was wearing a built-up shoe on her left foot, and when she stepped forward to shake hands, she limped. But the hand she held out was warm and strong, and when she took off her goggles, her eyes as well as her lips were smiling.

Josh turned to the tall girl. "Then, you're—" he began.

"I'm Crane,'' said the tall one. "I know you're sorry I'm not Helen.''

Now, how did she know that? All Josh could see of her was a pale face under a broad-brimmed hat. She wore a long, dark poncho that flopped around like a bat's wings whenever she moved. "Hi,'' she said briefly to G.G.

"I know I look funny,'' she added, again reading Josh's thoughts. "I have to keep covered. I burn.''

"Burn?'' Josh mumbled.

"Sunburn. It's one of my problems. I can't get brown. I just burn. I even have to have a veil, it's that bad. See?'' She unpinned a dark veil from the brim

22

of her hat. When it fell over her face, she was almost invisible in the gathering dark.

She scooped up the veil to pin it back on the brim of her hat and dropped the pin. Josh picked it up. It was shaped like a small black cat with shining green eyes. G.G. saw it too, and Josh heard him say under his breath, "A witch?"

3 ❀ ❀

A witch? Josh knew that G.G. was kidding, but all of his bad luck flashed through his mind. For a starter, Helen had not come on the trip. Then, he had busted his bike and lost his wallet. What if—? But there were no such things as witches, and anyway, this was Helen's sister, which automatically made her O.K. On the other hand, there were women who were trying to turn into witches. You read about them all the time. Maybe they started trying when they were young, and trying was certainly the way to succeed.

"Did you have any trouble finding Gitche Gumee?" asked Dusty.

"No," said Josh, "but I had plenty of other trouble." Again he told what had happened to him that day.

"Sounds dopey to me," said Crane. "I *thought* your bike looked busted. And you've only got three gears. We've all got ten. You'll never keep up."

So this was Helen's sister? Josh wondered to himself whether a broomstick had any gears. Why should he try to be nice to this girl? The trip hadn't even started and she was already insulting him. He said nothing, but determined then and there that he would not only keep up with the ten-gear bikes but would keep ahead.

Muff looked from Crane to Josh and back again. "Come on," she said cheerfully. "Chow." She led the way to a wooden table at the far side of the truck.

Josh saw a brick fireplace with a grill on which a black iron pot stood steaming.

"Get your plates and spoons," said Muff. "It's beans and hot dogs tonight. We can do the wieners on sticks over the fire."

When they had all gathered around, she ladled out the beans. "I'm just a plain cook, but Crane added some raisins to these beans," she explained. She handed out sticks and wieners.

"Raisins!" said Josh, looking at his plate suspiciously.

Crane peered into the pot and gave it a stir. "Yes, raisins. They give a wonderful flavor. Plain beans are so boring. You'll never eat plain beans again," she predicted.

But Josh and G.G. pushed the raisins to one side of their plates. First they ate the beans, then they ate the raisins.

"Beans are beans," G.G. said under his breath.

Josh agreed. "And raisins are raisins." Then he decided not to go looking for trouble with Helen's sister. "Nice try," he said.

Crane looked hurt, as if she had expected applause and cheers. However, they emptied the pot to the last bean, devoured the wieners, washed down with plenty of milk, and looked around for more. There were apples for dessert, and they too were gone in a flash, along with a package of cookies. Josh began wondering about breakfast even before they had finished supper.

"We should take turns cooking," Crane said. "Don't you think so?" And before anyone could say yes or no, she went on, looking around the circle and pointing her finger at each one, "Intery, mintery, cutery, corn/Apple seed and briar thorn." It was like a spell. "Wire, briar, limber lock,/Five geese in a flock,/Sit and sing by a spring,/And out goes Y-O-U." Crane's finger pointed at Josh. "So you'll cook breakfast."

Now *there* was a surefire way to get the trip off to a bad start for Josh and everyone else. "I can't cook," Josh said. "I've never cooked anything."

"Of course you can cook," Dusty said. "You can learn. Anyone can."

But Crane broke in. "If he doesn't want to, I'll take his turn. I'm a really good cook. I'll take your turn every time," she said to Josh. "You can do the cleaning up for me."

It sounded like a lot of K.P. duty, but he could stand it. "O.K.," he said, "as long as I don't have to cook. I'll start now."

There were faucets for cold water in the campground. Josh filled the black pot and set it on the grill to heat. Muff supplied soap powder and a scrubbing brush.

"But no towel," Dusty suggested. "K.P. is easy if you let everything dry by itself. And while you wash, the rest of the bunch can help me make camp."

From that evening on, Josh thought of them as the Bunch.

While he scrubbed the pot, the others untied a waterproof canvas that covered the rear of the truck. Dusty drove four metal poles into the ground and tied the canvas to the tops of the poles for a shelter. There was room under the shelter for four sleeping bags. Muff spread hers on the front seat of the truck. Then she lifted herself into the rear of the truck and called to Josh, "Bring me the plates and all that, will you? And take a look at the way Dusty has set things up here."

Josh dried his hands on the seat of his pants and came to look, carrying the pot and a pile of clean plates, cups, and spoons. He climbed up beside Muff.

"Neat-o," said Josh.

Behind the driver's cab was a wooden rack with room for four bikes. "When we all go in the truck, there will be room for two or three sitting on the floor back here, even with the bikes in the rack," Muff said.

A grocery carton held food supplies, and a shoe box was filled with road maps and manuals on bicycle care, first aid, and outdoor cooking. "That's the bare minimum that we need," Muff told Josh. "I wish we had more. But the rack is really good, isn't it? Dusty made the rack." From the way she said it, Josh knew that she liked Dusty a lot. Too bad she had that lame foot and the scar on her chin. Dusty ought to have a super girl, if he got interested.

The sound of a harmonica broke the silence. "That's Dusty," said Muff. "He's good, isn't he?"

Dusty was playing "I've Been Working on the Railroad" and Josh heard G.G. singing. Josh had sung at camp with Dusty, and he and G.G. knew the same songs from Oakley School. Dusty had been good on the ukulele at camp, and now Josh could tell he was even better on the harmonica. He was making it sound like ten Sousa bands. They should have some good singing on this trip.

Only G.G. was sitting with Dusty when Josh and Muff joined them, but a moment later Crane appeared out of the darkness, carrying a recorder. She plumped herself down, put the recorder to her lips, and sat waiting with raised eyebrows. When the chorus began, with its "Fee, fi, fiddley-i-o," Crane tootled along on the recorder, but she was out of tune and played more wrong notes than right ones. G.G. and Josh sang louder to drown her out.

From other campfires came complaints. "Pipe down! . . . Quiet!"

Dusty stopped playing, and the song came to a halt in the middle of a "fiddley-i-o."

"That's a boring song anyway," said Crane. She put her recorder to her lips again and began to play softly. Nobody sang.

After a while G.G. said, "That's a weird song."

"It isn't," Crane protested. "Listen. I'll teach it to you." She put down the recorder and launched into nine or ten verses that didn't make sense, as far as Josh could see. All he could make out was "Parsley, sage, rosemary, and thyme," over and over. He tried to start the canoe song he had learned at camp with

Dusty. Then he and G.G. tried "The fox went out on a chilly night," a glee-club favorite at school. But they couldn't turn Crane off. She went on and on with "Parsley, sage, rosemary, and thyme." She was playing it again on the recorder when he went with G.G. and Dusty to find the men's lavatory, where they could wash before bedtime.

Only Muff stayed to hear the end of Crane's song. On the way to the washroom, Dusty, Josh, and G.G. passed the camp store. Dusty bought three chocolate ice cream cones, which they polished off while they waited for their turns at the washbasins in the lavatory. G.G. picked up a joke book that someone had dropped and tried out a few jokes on Dusty and Josh. "Want to eat up the street? No, I hate concrete . . . Know how to catch a squirrel? Climb a tree and act like a nut." They took their time, laughing at the old jokes and talking. Being in the all-male lavatory was restful, Josh thought, after an evening with Crane.

When they came back to the truck, the fire in the fireplace had been doused and Muff had disappeared into the cab of the truck. Crane's sleeping bag looked so flat that Josh was not sure she was in it until her voice emerged from its depths. "And they say *girls* are slow!"

"We had some ice cream cones," Dusty said. "Want one?"

"Only if they have caramel," came the answer.

"There isn't any caramel," Josh told her.

"There never is." She made it sound as if it was his fault. Then she added, "If you're broke, let me know."

"I have plenty," he said stiffly.

When he had worked his way into his own sleeping bag, he thought he would try to figure Crane out before he went to sleep. With his eyes closed, he saw her finger pointing round and round the circle. How did that thing go? "Intery, mintery, cutery, corn . . ." And that song, "Parsley, sage, rosemary, and thyme," over and over. It could drive a guy nuts.

"Intery, mintery . . ." Josh got no further. He fell asleep as if he had been hit over the head by a hammer. Or charmed by a spell.

4 ❀ ❀

The next morning Josh woke because Dusty and G.G. were taking down the canvas. He felt the sun on his face and looked straight up into a sky already clear and blue. He had slept like a log.

Everyone else was up and out. Muff was putting plates and cups on the wooden table. Milk, cereal, and a can of orange juice stood ready. A small fire was beginning to crackle under the grill. Crane was nowhere to be seen. With a brief greeting to the others, Josh pulled on his pants and T-shirt.

G.G. was at work on his bike with the help of a monkey wrench and a paperback manual on the care and repair of bicycles. He swiveled his thumb to indicate the far side of the truck. "Step around and take a look," he said. Josh stepped around. Crane was sitting on the ground, her legs folded like a pretzel. Her hair hung down her back in a long braid.

"Oh, hi," Josh said.

"I can't talk, I'm meditating," she answered. She unfolded herself. Then she put her hands on the ground, palms up, rested the top of her head on her hands, and raised her feet until they were straight up in the air.

"Hey, look at that!" said Josh. Crane came crashing down to earth.

"You spoiled it," she said. "I always do yoga before breakfast, but I suppose you want to eat. Come on, then. I've picked berries. They're a lot better than that old canned juice."

Berries did sound better. Josh followed Crane back to the table, where the others were eyeing a small handful of berries on a tin plate.

"Crane's contribution," Muff said politely.

"What kind are they?" Josh wanted to know. They didn't look so hot after all.

"Blueberries—and other kinds," Crane said. She began to break eggs into the skillet. "You can eat practically any kind of berry."

"Not every kind," Muff said gently. "Some make you sick."

"Some kill you," G.G. said. "I don't eat berries

33

when I don't know what they are, you bet your life."

"I know what they are," Crane said, sounding offended. "If you don't want them, put them on my plate." She turned her back and stirred the eggs vigorously.

Josh munched his cereal and picked at the more familiar berries. Helen had told him to take care of Crane. If she poisoned herself on the first day of the trip, Helen wouldn't think he had done a very good job. Most of the berries were sour anyway. With winks and nods, Josh and G.G. dropped the strange ones on the ground. Presently Crane came with the skillet.

"Well," she said, seeing the almost empty plate, "I'm glad you all liked the berries. You're going to like the eggs too. Eat them while they're hot."

"What's that green stuff in them?" G.G. asked.

"Dandelions," said Crane, with a satisfied air. "I chopped them up to give a little flavor. You can add dandelions to almost anything."

Even Dusty, who generally took life and food any way it came, seemed to have trouble choking down the scrambled eggs and dandelions. However, he was never one to complain openly. He changed the subject. "About the trip for today. We'll be on a good road this morning, not too much traffic. We'll ride for an hour and then take a break. Around noon we'll stop again and have lunch at a quarry where we can swim. Muff will meet us there with the truck."

"What kind of a quarry?" Josh asked.

"A stone quarry," Dusty said. "They fill up with water sometimes. You'll see. Then we'll get on the shore road and follow it all the way to the dock. This is the day we go to the island, remember. We want to make the five o'clock boat."

Josh remembered. This should be one of the best parts of the trip, he thought. He had never seen saltwater or been in any boat bigger than a canoe. Moving fast, he packed his bike while the water for the dishes heated over the fire.

G.G. helped with the dishes. At least, he stood by and read jokes out of the old joke book, like "You're fresh . . . I'd rather be fresh than stale" and "Do you use toothpaste? . . . No, my teeth aren't loose." He was about to toss the joke book into a trash can when Muff saved it and tucked it into her book box. G.G. went off for a final check of his bike.

When the dishes and the sleeping bags had been stowed in the truck, Muff climbed into the driver's seat and started the motor. I, A TRUCK gave an asthmatic cough, emitted a cloud of blue smoke, and began to do a stately jig. Then came an agonized grinding of gears, Muff waved, and I, A TRUCK took off with a lurch.

"Do you think she'll make it?" Josh wondered aloud.

"Sure, she'll make it," Dusty said easily. "Muff always takes care of herself." He settled his Marine fatigue cap on his head and swung onto his bike saddle.

G.G. pulled a baseball cap with a red visor out of his pants pocket and wheeled off after Dusty.

"Follow me," Crane said. Josh stared at her. Crane was once again wearing her floppy poncho, and something new had been added under her big hat. From the top to the tip of Crane's nose ran a white Band-Aid. No matter how she looked, this was Helen's sister, but Josh was so full of things he wanted to say and didn't say that something was going to spill, sooner or later.

"I know what you're thinking," she said, tossing her braid behind her, "but I can't help it. My nose burns worst of all."

She set off along the dirt road through the campground, her braid swinging like a pendulum as she pedaled. Josh came last, grinning to himself. He had made up his mind what to do. As she turned into the main road, he passed her.

"See you," he called. She would find out that he could pass all of them on his three-speed bike.

The road ran mostly uphill, but now, after a good

night's sleep, hills were no problem. Josh's low gear was good enough for these gentle slopes. He soon caught up with G.G. and passed him with a wave. Ahead of Josh, Dusty rounded a bend in the road and disappeared briefly. Then Josh rounded the same bend and pulled even with him.

"Mind if I lead?" Josh called, and whizzed past.

He heard Dusty's "Take it easy," but he did not feel like taking it easy. It was great to be in the lead with the road all to himself. New sights opened out around every curve. The road wound through pine woods and oak woods. A blue pond sparkled behind a grove of slender white birch trees.

Josh sped along through patches of sun and shade, pedaling hard uphill and coasting down. With a year of school sports behind him—football, hockey, and crew—bicycling was a piece of cake. And now he was smelling something new in the air, something that he felt in his nose and in his blood. Above the earthy smells of the woods came a whiff of salt-sea smell. The sea was not far away. All of his life he had heard about it and read about it. Today he would see it with his own eyes and even sail on it. Yesterday's troubles were miles behind him. He had never felt so great. He could go on like this forever, speeding uphill and coasting down, getting nearer and nearer to the sea.

At the end of an hour he was not so sure that he

could go on forever. His leg muscles felt like spaghetti. His fingers were cramped from gripping the handlebars. Well, he had proved that he could set the pace any time he felt like it, and it was time for a break anyway. When he came to a shady slope of grass, he pulled off the road and flopped down, hot, sweaty, and thirsty, expecting to have a good rest and to cool off before the others arrived. But in no time at all, Dusty was swinging off his saddle beside Josh. A minute later came G.G., with Crane at his heels.

She sat down beside him, not at all winded, and held out a canteen, saying, "Have a drink."

Josh was thirsty enough to drink the ocean dry. He took a gulp. Then he blinked. It wasn't water. It wasn't anything he had ever tasted. He handed back the canteen. Had Crane poisoned him?

"It's hunnigar," she said. She took a big swallow. "Isn't it wonderful? There's nothing like it for a thirst. Finish it up, all of you. I can make plenty more."

"But what *is* it?" G.G. demanded, peering into the black hole of the canteen. "I'm not going to drink it if I don't know what it is."

"It's a secret," Crane told him, "but I swear it can't possibly hurt you. Go on, try it." She refused to say what the hunnigar was made of, so Dusty and G.G. preferred water from their own canteens. Josh lay down again. He was trying to decide whether or not he felt sick. The hunnigar had tasted both sweet and sour. It was certainly very good, but poisons often did taste good, or so he had heard.

Crane was exploring through the long grass and along the edge of the woods. Presently she came back with her hands full of green leaves.

"Here's something else that's good for thirst," she said. "Have some mint." Mint sounded safe enough. When Dusty and G.G. took some to chew, Josh decided to take a chance. He had already chewed and swallowed one leaf before Dusty spat his out, saying, "It looks like mint, but it doesn't taste like mint."

"Sure doesn't," G.G. agreed, frowning.

"Don't worry, it's mint," Crane reassured them. "At least, it's catnip."

Catnip! Josh had seen what catnip did to cats. Was he going to have fits too, and start meowing?

Dusty only laughed and wheeled his bike onto the road. "Thanks, but no thanks," he said. "By the way, Josh, really take it easy. Speeding and coasting is twice as hard. Find the pace that's right for you and hold it. There's no race."

Once again they were on the road, with Dusty in the lead, then G.G. with Crane following, and Josh bringing up the rear. With hunnigar and catnip inside him, he would be lucky if he didn't drop dead.

Following Dusty's advice, Josh kept a steady pace on the second leg of the day's journey. He didn't drop dead, and the going was easier, even though the sun was blazing toward noon. The only thing that bothered him was the sight of Crane, cycling ahead of him. He decided not to watch her braid as it swung left and right, left and right. That was how people got hypnotized.

At the top of a hill, Dusty halted the cavalcade. Josh saw a small grocery store and a filling station at the side of the road where Muff, in a swimming suit, was coming out from the door marked LADIES. Behind the filling station, I, A TRUCK was parked at the foot of a steep path. Looking up, Josh saw only a rim of rocks, but he knew that this must be the quarry where they would swim. He was hot and sticky and saddlesore. When he swung off his bike, his muscles felt stiff and aching. A swim would be great.

"I bought gas," Muff said, "so they're letting us change in their rest rooms. Come on. Let's swim." Her feet were bare, and without her built-up shoe, she limped more than ever, but she darted up the path faster than Josh could believe. When he came out with G.G. and Dusty from the room marked MEN and followed Muff, she was already in the water, swimming a fast and expert Australian crawl. Crane was in the water too, floating face up with her eyes closed.

40

"If that's all she does, she's a witch," Josh said privately to G.G. "Witches float. They can't drown."

Dusty didn't hear it. He had jumped into the water at once, but G.G. and Josh stood for a minute, looking into the quarry. Its rocky ledges surrounded a pool of the bluest water Josh had ever seen.

"It's warm," Dusty called. "Come on in."

"How deep?" Josh called back.

At once, Crane doubled up and disappeared beneath the surface. She did not come up.

G.G. began to count, ". . . eight, nine, ten . . . Do you think she's drowned?"

Drowned! Josh waited no longer. "Get Crane!" he shouted. He jumped, came to the surface, and took a deep breath, prepared to dive to the rescue. G.G. jumped in at the same moment. Then one of Crane's feet rose slowly from the water, pointed straight up, and turned slowly around, like a periscope. Next the foot went under water again, and Crane's head appeared. She shook the water out of her eyes and grinned.

"I couldn't find bottom, but how did you like my submarine trick?"

Dusty and Muff swam to Crane. She had scared all of them.

"Listen," said Dusty, treading water. "Don't play tricks under water when you don't know the bottom.

This quarry is deep, but you could hit your head. For Pete's sake, I have to take care of this Bunch."

Crane looked aggrieved. "I'm a senior lifesaver myself," she said. She climbed out on a rock, covered herself with her poncho, and lay as still as a corpse.

"Now she's mad," Josh said. He struck off across the quarry.

G.G., swimming beside him, sputtered, "Let her be."

But the water in the quarry, so deep, so warm, so blue, made everyone feel good again. Even Crane soon sat up, draped herself in her poncho, and went poking happily among the hilltop rocks.

It was G.G.'s turn to be the cook for lunch. He took the money Muff doled out and went down the hill to the grocery store, returning with peanut butter, jelly, a loaf of bread, and five candy bars.

"I wanted to get a carton of Cokes," he said, "but there wasn't enough money."

"Never mind Cokes," Muff told him. "We'll have hunnigar. I made lots of it."

"Hunnigar!" said Josh. "Did you make it? That's what Crane gave us. We thought it was one of her weird things."

Muff laughed. "It isn't weird, it's wonderful. We drink it on our farm when we cut the hay. It's the best thirst quencher in the world. Honey and vinegar mixed with water—hunnigar."

"I'll go and get Crane," Josh said. But although he clambered about among the rocks, looking, calling, whistling, there was no sign of Crane. It was not until he reached the edge of a little woods on the far side of the hill that he saw her, prowling along, bending down to pick something.

"What now?" Josh wondered.

"Mushrooms!" she said when she saw him, and held out a double handful. She sounded as if mushrooms were holy. "Have some."

"Raw?" Josh said. "Nothing doing."

"Of course, raw. They're delicious." She scooped one into her mouth. "Delicious. You're missing something."

Josh tried one. "Tastes like an eraser," he said. And again Crane looked wounded.

G.G. was slapping together some sandwiches when Crane and Josh came back to the quarry.

"Mushrooms for lunch," Crane announced hopefully.

"For your lunch, maybe," G.G. said. "Not for me. How do you know they aren't toadstools?"

"I just do know," Crane said defensively. "I know all about mushrooms."

Muff looked at Dusty, who shook his head.

"Crane," Muff said, *"we* don't know a thing about mushrooms. Some of them can be terribly poisonous. I feel responsible for all of you. Please don't eat them.

And please don't anyone else eat them. I want to get all of you home safely."

But even while she spoke, Crane was eating the mushrooms. She ate all of them. Like the rest of the Bunch, Josh ate peanut-butter-and-jelly sandwiches and a candy bar, washed down with hunnigar. He was no longer concerned about the hunnigar. But what about the mushroom he had eaten? For all he knew, Crane had given him a toadstool.

5 ✦✦

Josh, at the rear of the line again after lunch, caught up with the others not long after they had pulled off the road at the top of a hill for their first glimpse of the sea. G.G. and Crane lived near enough to the ocean to be able to take it for granted, but Josh and Dusty were landlubbers. Dusty was pointing to the east with one hand and waving Josh on with the other.

"That's it," Dusty was saying. Through half-closed eyes he looked at the sea as if he could never look his fill. Josh too stared eastward. Sandy hills tumbled down to a strip of golden beach and silvery surf. On a point of land a lighthouse stood, and beyond, to the horizon, lay one vast stretch of sparkling blue.

Josh drew a long breath and let it out in a silent whistle. However hard he looked, he could see only the near end of that ocean. This was the sea that circled the whole world, and somewhere beyond the horizon lay unknown lands. Maybe that was why it gave him a feeling like nothing he had ever felt. Saltwater! Before this trip was done, he would taste saltwater and swim in it. Before this very day was done, he would cross saltwater by boat to an island. He had never set foot on an island.

"Come on," he said. "Let's go."

"Right," said Dusty. "Muff's waiting, and we want to make that five o'clock ferry to the island." The words were offhand, but Josh could tell how excited Dusty was by the thought of that island.

"Keep to this road?" Josh asked. When Dusty nodded, he sprang to his saddle, gave his bike a kick as if he were spurring a horse to adventures, and pedaled off downhill. It was a steep hill, steeper than Josh had expected, and as he went down it, he gathered speed. Too late, he saw his mistake, put on his brakes, and held them on with all his strength. Ahead lay a spot where the wind had blown sand across the road. Josh hit that spot. His bike wobbled wildly, there was a swish, a thud, and for the second time in two days, he sprawled on the ground. He heard Dusty's voice, then G.G.'s, asking, "Are you O.K.?" and a moment later opened his eyes to see them looking down at him, their faces full of concern. Crane's pale face appeared above him briefly, but when he sat up, she was examining his bike and the contents of his basket, spilled over the road.

"You have a flat tire," she said. "I'll bet you haven't got a repair kit. Or if you have, you probably don't know how to fix a tire."

"I have a repair kit," he said, getting to his feet. But she was right. He had never mended a tire.

G.G. broke in, "For Pete's sake, Crane." Even Dusty frowned at her. Josh felt the Bunch coming apart at the seams. There were now three males against one female, a smaller Bunch, and Crane outside of it.

Then Dusty found the repair kit and said, "I've fixed plenty of tires and I've got a pump. This won't take long. Just keep off the road, out of traffic, while I do it."

He turned Josh's bike upside down, pried off the front tire, and found the leak. Then he set about applying a patch while Josh hovered, watching how it was done, and G.G. read advice from the Youth Hostels' handbook.

"We'll probably miss the ferry," Crane said

gloomily. She crossed the road and sat down with her back turned to them, her head bowed under the big hat, her arms clasped around her knees. She was always turning her back on them, it seemed.

"So help me, I'm going to take a poke at her one of these times," G.G. muttered.

Through Josh's mind flashed a series of pictures: G.G. poking Crane, Crane telling Helen, Helen blaming Josh, Josh trying to explain why he hadn't stopped G.G. from poking Crane, Helen never speaking to Josh again.

"Don't do it," he muttered in return. But if G.G. hadn't said it, he might have said it himself.

"Sit down and cool off," Dusty said, "before I take a poke at all of you." His voice was good-natured as always, but it cooled them off. G.G. had gotten a book of maps from Muff's "library." He and Josh put their heads together and studied it.

From across the road, Crane called, "I suppose you're talking about me."

"We're not," Josh called back and, thinking of Helen, added, "Come on over."

She came, slowly, but would not sit down.

Dusty was pumping up the mended tire. "Time to go anyway," he said. "I think we'll make the ferry."

Within an hour they were wheeling cautiously

through the crowded streets of a little waterside town and Dusty was asking the way to the docks. It was easy to get the answer because everyone seemed to be heading that way. The road ended in a wide parking area with sheds at the water's edge.

Then Josh saw the ferry, big, squat, and blunt-nosed. People were going on board, and cars, trucks, and trailers, many of them carrying bicycles, were driving into the hold at dock level. Josh spotted Muff, waving from her truck. I, A TRUCK, AM DOING THE BEST I CAN. Good old truck. It had made it, and Muff had made it, and all was well again.

Following Dusty's lead, Josh guided his bicycle into the dark hold, chained it to a post, and scrambled for the top deck. Haste was worthwhile, because they all got seats in the sun.

"Save ours for us," Dusty said. He signaled to Muff and they stood conferring privately at the rail. With the clank of chains, the toot of whistles, and the chatter and laughter of passengers, the ferry began to move out from shore. Josh could not hear what Dusty was saying, but he guessed that it was about his accident and the bad feelings afterward.

The ferry nosed out beyond the last point of the mainland, past low-lying islands and into deep water. Above the steady chug of the engine, Josh heard the slap-slap of whitecaps breaking against the sides of the ferryboat. There was spray in the air, too fine to see, but enough to taste on his lips. Saltwater! In the late sunshine, gulls circled overhead.

Presently, Muff handed out cookies and curled up on a deck chair beside Josh. Dusty lay down on the deck to sleep, his fatigue cap over his eyes. Josh and G.G., who were always famished, devoured their cookies at once, but Crane nibbled as if she had no appetite.

Above them the gulls, gray-backed, yellow-beaked, dipped and soared, dipped and soared. The sun shone through the edges of hovering wings. Josh, looking up at the gulls, saw their white-feathered breasts, their neat little feet pointed and held close under fan-shaped tails.

"Like landing gear," he said, to no one.

"Ballet," said Crane.

A gray-bearded man was standing at the bow of the ship, a man with a cowboy hat and khaki shorts, and knobbly knees. He held up his hand to feed the gulls, and the gulls flew to him. They took the food from his fingers as they flew. Crane saw it. She jumped up and picked her way among the passengers to stand beside the stranger. Then she reached up on tiptoe, her hand stretched skyward. What did she think she was now, a ballet dancer? Josh wondered. He saw a gull floating toward her on a current of air, taking a cookie crumb from her fingers, and swooping away.

"Look at that!" he exclaimed to G.G. "She can't get along with people, but she sure gets along with birds."

Then he saw Crane talking to the stranger. This man could be some kind of a creep. Josh nudged G.G. "Watch that guy," he said. "If he does anything funny, I'm going to jump him. Help me, will you? I'm supposed to take care of Crane because she's Helen's sister."

"Right," said G.G., "even if she is a weird sister." They doubled up with laughter, while Crane and the stranger went on feeding the gulls.

Muff, who had seemed to be napping, came to life. "I hear you had a bad spill this afternoon," she said to Josh. "Hope you didn't get hurt."

"Not too much," he told her.

"But Dusty says that Crane made everybody mad, the way she acted."

"For no reason," G.G. contributed. "I said all along she was a witch, and that was how she acted this afternoon."

"She might turn into one," Muff said, "depending on how you and Josh treat her. Take a shy person, especially a smart one, let her feel lonely, make her think you don't like her, and you've got half a witch right there."

"Don't like her?" Josh protested. "I've been trying

to take care of her the whole time, but she's always picking on me for some reason."

"I don't know the reason," Muff answered, "but look at it this way. You and Dusty knew each other before this trip started. You knew G.G. at school. Dusty and I met before the trip, and we're older, anyway. When we started, everybody knew somebody, except Crane. She was nobody's special friend. And now we're a Bunch, as we keep saying. But Crane isn't quite in the Bunch, yet, and until she is, she'll probably get worse and spoil the trip for all of us, including herself. Try looking at her a new way, somehow."

Squinting into the sun, Josh looked at Crane again. The stranger was sitting on the deck, reading a paperback book. Crane was still at the bow, and the gulls, above the darkening water, were still flying to her, one after another, to feed from her hand. Josh had to admit it was a pretty thing to see. It almost made him think of the way he had first seen Helen, skimming toward him over the ice on the river at school, her arms outstretched, her hair flying in the wind. Of course, Crane wasn't Helen, but at this moment he could see that she really was Helen's sister. If you looked at her that way.

He was just deciding to look at her that way from now on when she turned around and looked at him, big hat, floppy poncho, Band-Aid, and all.

"There's the island!" she called. All the other passengers turned to see who her friend was. Josh sat silent and tried to pretend he wasn't the one. Crane was not Helen after all. She was a weird sister.

6 ✸ ✸

Josh woke Dusty in time, so that he could see the island nearing above the horizon. What looked at first like a thin black line soon widened into a view of hills and cliffs and a town where white houses clustered around a wharf like the one they had left an hour ago. Dusty called the Bunch together.

"Take a look at your maps," he said. "We're headed for the island youth hostel. Now we might get separated in traffic or miss the road, but this hostel is one of the biggest and best anywhere, and almost any islander can tell you where it is, from what I've heard. See, you turn left at the end of the wharf, then right up the hill, then like this, and this, and you're there."

The boat whistle gave a long blast, and bicyclists and motorists made for the hold. Muff squeezed back into the truck, and all waited impatiently for the moment of landing. At last they heard the welcome rattle of chains; the landing gear moved into place, and the exit began. Bicycles seemed to have multiplied on the ferryboat, like animals coming out of the ark. Josh saw at least a dozen he hadn't noticed before, and their riders pushed off at once. Dusty grinned. "I guess most of them are headed for the hostel too. It ought to be quite a night."

The road to the hostel had looked easy on the map, but as Dusty had guessed, the Bunch were soon separated by traffic in the town. Not long after Josh had turned left at the end of the wharf and right up the hill, and tried to make the other turns, he found himself alone at the edge of town with the unknown island ahead of him. He asked for directions from one passerby after another, but none of them was an islander. Josh kept getting answers like "I'm a stranger here myself" or "Sorry, I just got off the ferry."

Josh was standing beside his bike, peering at his map, feeling lost and slightly "panicked," when a man's voice said, "Looking for the hostel?" Josh looked up and saw the bearded stranger with the cowboy hat.

Should he say yes, no, or jump on his bike and take off at full speed? This man could be the kind of stranger his mother had meant when she said, "Don't talk to strangers." But Crane had talked to him and survived.

Then the man came close and put a tanned finger on the map. Josh thought of headlines: BEARDED STRANGER KIDNAPS BICYCLIST.

"You're here," said the bearded one. "Go on to the fork in the road. Then keep to the right. The hostel will be straight ahead about a mile. I'll see you there." He stepped back, shifting the pack on his back for comfort.

After all, Josh thought, this old guy with a pack on his back could hardly chase a guy with a bike. He swung onto his saddle, then, with a sudden return of suspicion, asked, "How did you know I was looking for the hostel?"

"Your friend Crane told me. I saw you on the ferry."

"Oh," said Josh. Then, indicating his loaded bicycle, "Sorry I can't give you a ride." He hoped he sounded cool and casual.

"That's all right," the man said, laughing. "I always walk. I take shortcuts, and I'll be there almost as soon as you are, maybe sooner."

Josh followed the stranger's directions and found,

to his surprise, that he had arrived not at some sinister den but at the hostel. It was big and rambling, built of logs, and standing on a wide lawn. Bicycle racks, full of bikes, stood by the door, and at the end of the driveway I, A TRUCK was parked among several station wagons and trailers. Through the hostel's lighted windows Josh saw a crowd of people milling around. When he opened the door, other hostelers were lined up at a desk, signing in, and among them was the bearded stranger. Josh couldn't believe it.

"You beat me," he said.

The bearded one only smiled, said, "Shortcuts," and walked away.

Josh picked up the pen to sign in and looked at the last name on the list. It was Amos Walker. Walker— that made him more mysterious than ever.

There were other grownups at the hostel too. Josh saw that hostelers, like campers, came in all sizes, shapes, colors, and ages, except young children. A young man and woman introduced themselves as Mac and Mrs. Mac, houseparents for the hostel. They gave Josh a warm welcome, put a set of hostel rules in his hand, and told him he'd find Dusty in the boys' dorm.

Josh went to look for the Bunch. He crossed a big, barnlike room where some hostelers were cooking at a row of stoves. Others were eating at long wooden tables, while a few were on K.P. duty, taking turns at the sinks.

As predicted, Josh found Dusty in the boys' dormitory. He was sitting on a bunk, changing his socks.

"The hostel is full," he said. "Lucky we had a reservation. G.G. is having a shower, and you can too, if you want one. By that time we should be able to get a stove and table. I'm the cook tonight. Muff is on K.P. And there's a square dance afterward in the common room. Or Ping-Pong, if you don't want to dance."

A hot shower felt wonderful to sore muscles, and Dusty's beef stew, out of cans, hit the spot for empty stomachs. With fresh tomatoes, a long loaf of crusty bread, and plenty of milk, it was a feast fit for a king, especially when Muff brought out cold watermelon slices for dessert. Even Crane liked it. She said it was the first civilized meal they had had on the trip.

"And real beds tonight." G.G. sighed with satisfaction. "I can't wait."

"But first the square dance," Crane reminded him.

"I want to play Ping-Pong," he said, and asked Josh, "How about a couple of games?"

"I'd just as soon play too," Dusty agreed.

"Then good night," Crane said, and flounced off to the girls' dormitory.

"Go and get her," Dusty said to Muff. "Let's all give the dance a whirl. We can play Ping-Pong tomorrow."

While they waited for the girls, he took a copy of the hostel rules from his pocket and read them over with G.G. and Josh. "No food or drinks in the dormitories. Keep the bunks clean. Hostel chores will be assigned by the houseparents . . . H'm, chores. Sweep dorms. Wash down showers. Wipe sinks. Pick up trash . . . There are lots of chores. We should sign up for our share."

Then Muff returned alone, looking upset. "Crane won't come to the square dance," she said. "She thinks nobody likes her."

The three boys looked helplessly at Muff. At that moment they heard the sound of a guitar being tuned, and someone at a piano in the common room began to play "Chopsticks." Other hostelers were drifting from all parts of the hostel toward the common room.

"Go on," Muff said. "I'll do K.P. And you might as well give up on Crane."

"I'll help you," Dusty told her, but she shook her head. "It's no problem. Go on. That's an order."

"Who are we supposed to dance with?" G.G. asked of nobody in particular.

"Anybody," Muff said, clattering plates. "At a square dance it doesn't matter. You can even dance with yourselves."

The three exchanged dubious glances and took themselves off.

"Is Muff mad at us too?" Josh asked. "We didn't do anything."

"Who knows?" G.G. shrugged. "Sometimes females act that way for no reason."

"There's a reason," Dusty said. "We just didn't get it in time. They want to dance."

With G.G. and Josh he stood in the doorway of the common room, surveying the scene. Ping-Pong tables had been pushed to one side, and chairs were out of the way in a row against a wall to clear the floor for dancing. Mrs. Mac was at the piano in the far corner of the room, swinging into some country-style music. The guitar player turned out to be Mac, who now shouted above the hubbub of the milling hostelers.

"Take your partners for 'Golden Slippers.' Don't hold back, get on the track. This is easy, simple and breezy. Do-si-do, come on, let's go."

"Hey, look who came!" G.G. exclaimed.

In a square of dancers forming near a back door was Crane. Gone were the hat, the Band-Aid, the poncho. Crane's hair was unbraided, and her feet were bare. She was wearing something that looked like a nightgown.

It *is* a nightgown, Josh thought. No other girl in the room looked like that. Crane's partner was Amos Walker, with his cowboy hat.

Josh and G.G. moved purposefully across the room.

They leaned against the wall as near to Crane as they could get and kept their eyes on the old geezer with the cowboy hat.

Mac called out the steps of "Golden Slippers," and the dancers walked through the steps without music. "The first young man with the fair young maid/Go down the center and promenade./The lady go right, the gent go left./And balance to your partner./And now you all go do-si-do./And swing the gal that you don't know./Swing her high and swing her low./And then you promenade . . ."

It looked easy. Josh saw Dusty talking to Muff. He held out his hand to her. She smiled, but she shook her head. They sat down side by side. No dancing for Muff. And suddenly Josh knew that Muff wanted to dance even more than Crane did.

Then the music began again and the dancers moved with it, round in a circle and round again. Weaving in and out, stepping forward, stepping back. The music moved faster and dancers' faces became intent as they tried to get the steps right. Crane was getting them right. Now she bowed to her partner and he bowed to her. She looked solemn, but supremely satisfied.

"I'll get her for the next dance," Josh said determinedly. "Then you get her. She ought to stick with our Bunch." G.G. nodded.

When the music stopped, Josh closed in on Crane.

"I'll dance the next one with you," he said. But before he had finished saying it, another hosteler had taken her hand and led her away. He was big and fat, maybe a college guy, Josh guessed. He and G.G. were left holding up the wall through that dance. By turns, they tried to get Crane for dance after dance, but others always got her first. Josh was not sure whether they chose her or she chose them.

"Some square dance," G.G. said. "We might as well have played Ping-Pong."

Mac called, "Everyone on the floor for the Grand March, and that's all for tonight." He put down his guitar. He would need both hands to direct the Grand March.

Mrs. Mac began to play "Stars and Stripes Forever." The fat college guy roared out, "Be kind to our four-footed friends, for that duck may be somebody's mother . . ." Everyone joined in. Nobody wanted to sit this one out. Even Muff could walk through a Grand March. Josh saw her standing hand in hand with Dusty as pairs began to form and to march around the room. Josh and G.G. would have to be a pair, but Muff had said that didn't matter at a square dance. Two by two, all the hostelers circled the room.

Mac waved the pairs to the left or the right as they passed him, and the next march around was four by four. Then eight by eight. When the eights joined

into two lines of sixteen straggling, pulling, tugging hostelers, Josh found Crane's hand in his. The fat guy had her other hand. On the final go-round, Mrs. Mac was pounding her heart out on the piano and one long line snaked its way around the room. The fat guy, whooping and hollering, was making the snake whip. Dusty hauled Muff to safety on the sidelines while there was still time.

"Stop pulling me!" Crane cried above the uproar.

"I can't help it! Hang on!" Josh yelled.

But she let go instead. At the same time, Josh lost G.G.'s hand. He was catapulted out of the Grand March and onto a Ping-Pong table.

Everyone was shouting, "You may think that this is the end. And it is . . ."

And it was. The Grand March was over. They were all laughing at Josh, spread-eagled on the Ping-Pong table. It had been fun while it lasted, but Josh felt like a fool. He always seemed to end up a loser, trying to take care of Crane.

At ten thirty the tired hostelers gladly settled down in the two dorms. Josh saw Amos Walker laying out a sleeping bag on a bunk opposite his own. He seemed to be watching Josh. Even after lights out, Josh had a feeling of eyes staring from that opposite bunk. He hoped this old guy was not going to be hanging around the Bunch the rest of the way, hanging around

Crane. She was the kind of nut who would like Walker better than someone her own age. She would probably go off with Walker, just for kicks, if he asked her. And she'd never be seen again. Well, Josh would not let that happen. First thing in the morning, he would tell Walker to shove off.

7

When Josh opened his eyes the next morning, he thought he was the first one awake in the boys' dorm. Then he saw that Amos Walker's bunk was empty. At the foot of his own bunk lay the cowboy hat. Josh tumbled out of bed, pulled on his pants, and, taking the hat with him, went to look for the owner. But Amos Walker was gone.

Josh found Mac already busy at the registration desk. "Walker left his hat, did he? Maybe he'll come back for it. He left early," Mac said.

"He won't come back," said Crane, appearing at Josh's elbow. She had a new Band-Aid on her nose and looked dejected. "We'll never see him again. Ships that pass in the night, that's all we were."

Mac nodded sympathetically. "Right. Especially when you're hosteling, you meet people you'd like to know better and then they're gone."

"Walker is a real wizard," Crane said.

Wizard! "What do you mean—wizard?" Josh asked suspiciously.

"I mean he knows *everything!*" Crane said passionately. "Everything I want to know and to do. He once walked all the way from Georgia to Maine, and now he's walking back to Georgia."

"I don't believe it," Josh said.

"You wouldn't. But of course he did it. And do you know why?" Crane looked scornfully at Josh. "No, you wouldn't. He did it just to enjoy nature. Now he's on his way south with the birds. He knows all the birds. In one day, he was my friend. And I'll never see him again."

Josh pointed to the cowboy hat. "If he isn't coming back, why did he leave this? Did he just forget it?"

"He left it for you," Crane said. "He told me you ought to have a hat for sun and rain."

Josh was speechless. He had started this trip feeling suspicious of strangers, and with reason. The first day had proved that. But now he had been suspicious of a stranger who had done no harm, and had even done him a good turn. It was too late to apologize to Amos Walker or to thank him, but he would wear the cowboy hat, remembering from now on that not all strangers were necessarily creeps.

Among the last of the sleepers to waken was G.G. He too found a present from Amos Walker on his bunk. It was a paperback book called *The Hobbit*. G.G. read the first chapter while he ate his breakfast.

"It's good," he said. "These guys are peaceful, they like home, they hate war and all that stuff. But this one hobbit gets a great idea. He leaves home and starts off for an adventure. And listen to this about hobbits' feet . . ."

"Everybody has read that book," Crane interrupted. "The next time I take a trip, I'm going to walk. Like a hobbit. Like Walker. He said always walk proud, shoulders back, head up. But walk comfortably. Wasn't that great? He was a real wizard." She looked accusingly at Josh and G.G. "He gave you presents, and you didn't even like him."

"I just thought . . ." Josh searched for a way to explain, and found one of Crane's own expressions. "I just thought it would be a bore to have a stranger hanging around our Bunch all the way."

"A bore!" Crane cried. "Who's a bore?" She glared at Josh and G.G. "You never want to let an outsider in. That's the way you are. You're a bore!"

She certainly could make you feel like two cents. However, there was no time to brood over grievances. After breakfast all the hostelers packed their bikes and cars and did their hostel chores. G.G. swept the dining room. Dusty washed down a shower stall. Muff and Crane swept the girls' dorm. Josh cleaned a stove that was generously decorated with samples of last night's supper and this morning's breakfast. By nine thirty in the morning all chores were finished and the hostel was empty. All the travelers were on the road.

"What a morning!" Dusty said, squinting into the light. "There's a town about five miles north. We'll buy some food and see the sights there. Then we can go on to the beach for a picnic and a swim. We'll take the last ferry back to the mainland tonight. I wish we could stay here. There's something about an island . . ."

Josh saw Muff smile at Dusty, but all she said was, "I'll buy gas and park the truck at the first filling station I see when we come to town. Watch for me and the truck." I, A TRUCK chugged away, and the bicyclists followed.

Riding a bicycle on a morning like this, in a place like this, was so fine that even fighting with Crane couldn't spoil it. The air was soft and fresh, the island was basking in warm sunlight, and Josh's eyes under the brim of the cowboy hat took in low stone walls and fields of berry bushes. A line of ducks were paddling among cattails at the edge of a pond. The bicycles passed a lagoon where small boats were anchored. Then the white spire of a church rose above distant trees and there was the little town. There too was I, A TRUCK getting gas at a filling station.

When the Bunch had gathered, Muff said, "Stash your bikes in the truck. Dusty and I can shop for groceries while the rest of you explore. We'll meet you back here in an hour."

All hands helped to hoist the four bikes into the truck and chain them to Dusty's bicycle rack, after which the Bunch went their separate ways. Dusty and Muff headed for a supermarket. The ride had made Josh feel hollow with hunger. Looking for a good snack that wouldn't cost too much, he straggled after G.G. and Crane through narrow streets crowded with cars and bicycles. They drifted in and out of little shops, toy shops, book shops, gift shops, and wandered into traffic as if the island were under a good spell and no one would think of running them down.

Suddenly Crane darted across the street under the very nose of an oncoming car. "Wait for me!" she called, and disappeared into an old barn where a sign read NATURAL FOODS.

"There she goes again," G.G. groaned. "I know what those places sell—fried grasshoppers. Double, double, toil and trouble."

Josh had spotted what he wanted, a shop that sold thirty flavors of ice cream. G.G. followed, and they concentrated on making the right choice as they waited in line for cones. It seemed ages until their turn came, ages during which Josh noticed the high price of these fancy cones, realized the foolishness of spending emergency money for luxury ice cream, and decided that this *was* an emergency. Ever since the start of the trip, he had spent a little here and a little there for snacks. It was surprising how fast the money went. But if he didn't get something to eat, now, fast, he would be dead. He wanted all thirty flavors.

He might never have settled on one flavor, but G.G. saved the day by saying, "Chocolate chip," and Josh thankfully ordered, "The same."

They emerged from the ice cream shop blissfully licking the cones and saw Crane across the street, waving to them to come. She looked very pleased until she saw the cones.

"I don't suppose you got one for me?" she said, sounding as if she knew the answer.

"There wasn't any caramel," said Josh.

"Thirty flavors and no caramel." Crane sniffed.

"Never mind. I'm buying honey for all of us, and there are bees! In a glass hive! Come and see them."

They followed her into the barn. There were no other customers, only a girl pottering around an ancient cash register.

"See!" Crane purred happily. She pointed to jars of herbs that lined the walls. "Parsley, sage, rosemary, and thyme! They're all here. And there's the hive."

The beehive looked like a glass box. A glass pipe through the wall of the barn connected the hive with outdoors, and bees were crawling in and out through the pipe. The entire hive was filled with honeycomb and thousands of bees.

"Look!" said Crane. "That's what I call a perfect society, a perfectly natural society. Our society should be like that. But it isn't. It's rotten."

Josh had picked up a sheet of information about the bees. "It says here," he told Crane, "that the female bees do all the work. From now on, you can do all the work, Crane. How about that?"

G.G. hooted with laughter while Crane snatched the information sheet. She read quickly, frowning. "*But*," she said triumphantly, "the queen bee is the head of the whole hive and the males are drones. They're good for nothing except to mate with the queen bee, it says here. And she only chooses the best." Crane picked up a jar of honey and flounced over to the cash register. Josh and G.G. understood from this that they were drones and that if they were the last drones in the world, Crane would not choose them. They looked at each other and laughed.

"You think you're a queen?" Josh challenged her. "You sure don't act like one."

"We may be drones," G.G. chortled, "but you're just a plain female worker. Hey, Crane, when we get on the road again, you can carry all our stuff on your bike."

Crane scurried out of the barn and headed for the filling station, followed by the two boys, who were still laughing. They finished their chocolate-chip cones in high good humor.

Muff and Dusty were ready and waiting when they reached the filling station and changed into their swimming suits. Then Crane jumped into the seat of the cab, looking upset and paler than ever. "I want to ride with you, Muff," she said.

As they rode to the beach in the back of the truck with the bikes, Josh and G.G. told Dusty the joke about the bees. Dusty didn't think it was a very funny joke.

"Watch it," he said. "Kidding is all right, but some people can't take much of it, and Muff thinks Crane can't. You'd better lay off. We want this trip to be a good one for everybody."

"But she starts it," Josh said.

"Even so," Dusty answered, "Muff says you should lay off the kidding."

I, A TRUCK stopped, and Dusty changed the subject in his usual friendly way. "Look! Here's the beach. There's a lifeguard, but let's stick together anyway."

They spilled out among other parked trucks and cars, and ran onto a wide stretch of deep golden sand. Josh floundered through it to the edge of the sea. Here the beach was packed hard and smooth by the surge of saltwater. Josh ran faster. He splashed into white foam, scooped up a handful of water, and tasted. It was salt, all right! Saltier than tears, and with an extra taste besides. One taste was enough. He would keep his mouth shut, once he started swimming. He ran deeper into the water, flailing his arms to keep his balance. The water surged around him and pulled him back toward the beach. Then it pulled him in deeper again. There was something powerful out there in the ocean.

At Camp Buddy, Josh had swum in a quiet lake where the water hardly moved. In the river at Oakley School, the water flowed all one way and you knew which way you were going when you swam there. The ocean was something else. Beyond the ebb and flow of the waves that broke on the shore, there were bigger waves that had rolled in from thousands of miles away, and suddenly Josh felt afraid of them. He definitely did not want to get out beyond his depth.

G.G. didn't look scared. He was already swimming in deeper water. Now Muff and Crane were plunging in.

"Here goes," called Dusty, and made a surface dive. He reappeared beside Josh with a grin, wiping salt-water from his eyes.

Josh took a big breath and leaned forward for a surface dive. At that moment a wave hit him and knocked him over backward. He gasped, swallowed a mouthful of saltwater, and the sea closed over his head. Choking and spluttering, he struggled to right himself and to get his feet on solid bottom again. Then he felt a hand pulling him to the surface. It was Crane's hand. When he opened his eyes, stinging with salt, he saw that she was laughing at him. "You looked so funny! When a wave comes, dive under. The water is smooth when you're deep down."

Josh turned his back on her without answering. If someone had to help him, why did it have to be Crane? He waded to the beach and found a warm hollow, far back from the water, where the sand was deep and dry. There he lay down and closed his eyes. He felt battered, as if he had lost a fight with some huge thing. The others were all riding the waves and diving through them like whales. But Josh's first encounter with the sea had made him look foolish again. He would rest awhile before he had another go at it.

Presently, when he felt better, he went back to the edge of the water where little kids were playing. He would sit there for a while and get used to the waves before having another swim. First he sat, half in and half out of the water. At last he lay down, his body washed gently by the coming and going of the waves as they rose and fell on the beach. This was great. Now he was ready for a real swim.

Josh stood up. Then he clutched his swimming trunks. They weighed a ton. They bulged and sagged. While he had rocked back and forth in the shallow water, his suit had filled with sand. If Crane saw him now, she'd laugh her head off. Bowlegged with his load of sand, Josh waddled into the sea. But as he began to swim, Crane came riding on the crest of a wave, calling, "I saw you! Oh, you looked so funny!"

Josh didn't answer. She let him have it every time, and if he couldn't give it back, he was going to bust. He kept on swimming, while one by one, the rest of the Bunch left the water and went to stretch out on the sand.

"We'll watch you," Dusty said, "but don't get out too far."

Josh swam until he was sure that all of the sand had

been washed out of his swimming trunks. He took the waves as they came. He swam into deeper water where he could dive under as the waves towered over him. Deep down, as Crane had said, the water was smooth. Each time he dived deep, a flowing mountain of water passed over him and he came safely out on the far side of the wave. When his dive was not deep enough, he took a beating from the riot of water, as the waves pummeled him, and shook him, and scraped him over the sand. But Josh continued to dive. He knew that the others were watching. At least Dusty was. Maybe Crane was too.

Finally Josh left the water and marched up the beach to join the Bunch. He had lost his first round with the sea, but he had held his own in the second round. No matter what Crane said, he felt pretty good. He flopped down on the sand.

Crane had anointed herself with sunburn oil and pulled down the veil on her big hat for extra protection. She said nothing to anyone until it was time to leave the beach. One by one, the others went to change their clothes in the truck. Crane waited until all but Josh had gone. Then she said, "I'm sorry I was mean. I know I have been all along. When I was riding up in front with Muff, she told me I had to apologize."

Josh was too surprised to find a good answer. All he could mumble was, "O.K."

76

"I was really just kidding, most of the time," Crane went on. "But I know you like Helen and I know you don't like me that much, at least not now. There's no reason why you would."

Josh was already red with sunburn. He turned redder. "I'll be friends if you will," he said.

Crane's voice came softly from under her veil. "I want to. I like you a lot." On the brim of the big hat, the green-eyed cat winked in the sunlight. It looked as innocent as a kitten.

8 ❀ ❀

A week later, at a lake three hundred miles farther north, the Bunch, soaked to the skin in spite of ponchos and raincoats, holed in at the Big Pine Youth Hostel, waiting for the end of an all-day rain that looked like Noah's flood.

They had stayed at a different hostel or camp each night, and no two were alike. This one had six small cabins and a big main cabin. Letters or cards had been waiting there for everyone. Josh was the luckiest one. In a small package from his mother was a letter and his wallet with all the money he had thought was G-O-N-E. The letter said,

78

Dear Josh,

No postcards from you so far, but I've had some news about you anyway. Mr. Lowe wrote from Oakley School that you had had an accident and lost your wallet. He went back to the house where the accident happened and gave the people your name. Then he went to the police station and reported the loss of your wallet. The police had it! A stranger had turned it in, and all the money was there. I'll have to take back what I said about strangers, at least some of them. This proves that there still are some honest people in the world. Mr. Lowe sent your wallet safely home. I hope you will get safely home too and I hope you are having a good time.

Love from your ever anxious Mother.

Josh spread the good news and bought a postcard with a picture of little boats under a blue sky sailing on a blue lake surrounded by mountains. He stretched out before the fire in the main cabin to dry his clothes and wrote on the back of the postcard, as small as possible: "Dear Mother, That was lucky about my wallet. I wish I could thank whoever turned it in. Big Pine Lake would look like this if it ever stopped raining. I am fine. Love, Josh."

That used up all the space. There was no room left

79

to tell about the trip. To tell it all would fill a book. Josh had traveled a long way since leaving home, sometimes on his bike, sometimes in the truck, and every mile had been full of adventure. He closed his eyes and tried to remember it all. His accident in Rivertown seemed a long time ago. So did the first night when he had met the Bunch at Gitche Gumee Campground. The trip on the ferryboat, the swim through the surf on the island, all seemed a long time ago.

Every day Josh was seeing things he had never seen before, things maybe two hundred years old. One day the road had led through an old covered bridge, the kind that Josh had never expected to see except in picture books. Once they found an ice house and scrambled up a wooden ladder to look in through a high opening. All they could see was sawdust, but they knew that it covered the winter's ice from New England lakes and kept it frozen through the hot days of summer. A man had opened a bottom door and dug out chunks of ice for the Bunch to suck.

While they were quenching their thirst, a long line of bicyclists had passed. Josh counted eighty and then lost track. The Bunch shouted questions, and the bicyclists shouted back that they were a Bike-a-thon. Each one had paid a fee to raise money for a children's hospital. One girl wore a nurse's uniform and rode a giant tricycle. Another was a girl perched high on a unicycle. Several pairs were riding tandems. There was no telling all that Josh had seen on this trip. Before it began, he had lived in a very small world. Even when he had left home to go to camp and to boarding school, it was still a small world where he could be pretty sure what would happen and each day was almost like the next. On a bicycle trip, anything could happen and no day was like the next.

Crane still caused plenty of trouble, and it was hard to take care of her, but he was still trying. She said she liked him and then got mad at him when she should be grateful. She knew an awful lot, but she still acted dumb, like last night.

They had stayed at a camp in a woods. The big attraction there was a garbage dump where a mother bear and her cub were said to be regular visitors. Crane went into a tailspin when she heard that. She went rushing off to see if it was true, and Josh followed. They found the dump and a small round furry bear cub pawing and sniffing about, exactly as promised.

"Winnie-the-Pooh!" Crane sang out, like an idiot. Josh jerked her braid just as she was bending over the cub, arms outstretched, about to hug it. Crane was furious with Josh, but he held on to the braid and pulled her back by main force, pointing to the edge of the woods where the mother bear was advancing to the defense of her cub with a growl and a menacing gleam in her eye.

Josh's heart was hammering against his ribs and his mouth was dry as he hauled Crane away, warning, "You leave bears alone, especially a mother with a cub."

Crane only said, "Let go. Nothing would have happened. She liked me. You didn't have to jerk my head off." And she went into a sulk.

You never knew what crazy thing she would do next, but she certainly had the Bunch under her spell. She still stood on her head every morning and they had all learned to do it too. She still put weird things into the food every time she got a chance, but some of Crane's wild food was good. Bicycling and fresh air made almost anything taste good. Once, in a woods, Crane had found some May apples, oval and golden yellow. She showed Josh how to squeeze them between his fingers and shoot the juice right into his mouth. It tasted like strawberries. At night Crane played the recorder. Now they all knew "Parsley, sage, rosemary, and thyme," and she was teaching them a song about the keys to Canterbury.

"O madam, I will give you the keys to Canterbury,
And all the bells of London will ring to make us
    merry,

If you will be my bride, my sweet and only dear,
And walk along with me anywhere."

Josh and G.G. and Dusty were supposed to sing that part, but they always messed it up, on purpose. Then Crane and Muff sang:

"O sir, I'll not accept from you the keys to Canterbury,
Though all the bells of London should ring to make
us merry,
I will not be your bride, your sweet and only dear,
And walk along with you anywhere."

Like all of Crane's songs, this one went on and on. The guy was always offering to give the girl something and she said she didn't want it. Finally, he said he would give her a long dress, and she liked that.

"O sir, I will accept from you a braw, braw silken
gown,
With nine yards a-trailing, a-trailing on the ground,
And I will be your bride, your sweet and only dear,
And walk along with you anywhere."

Dusty was learning to play "The Keys to Canterbury" on his harmonica. It passed the time in the evenings. Josh wondered if Dusty thought about Muff when he played that song, the way Muff thought about Dusty. Everyone else could see how much Muff liked Dusty, but it was hard to tell whether Dusty even noticed. Both were good hostelers, trying to make everything go well for the Bunch, no matter how they were feeling themselves. That was all Josh knew.

G.G. was a good hosteler too and always did more than his share of the work. At first he had kept everyone laughing with terrible puns and riddles from the old joke book. "Cross a hobo with a deck of cards and get a bum deal . . . Name six things smaller than an ant's mouth. Six of its teeth." But now at night he entertained them by telling the plot of *The Hobbit,* in installments. He had become an expert at bicycle repairs too and took his bike apart almost every evening. Josh didn't dare to do that. He knew he would have nuts and bolts left over when he tried to put things together again.

Another thing that made this trip so great was meeting new people every night. It was no longer possible for Josh to think of any hostelers or campers as strangers. They were all on the same sort of journey. They might meet for only one evening—ships that passed in the night, as Crane put it—but most became friends right away. There was always fun and good talk, of bicycling, of hiking or backpacking, of canoeing, and of rafting along rivers. Someday, Josh thought, he himself would travel all these ways. With closed eyes, he saw roads leading everywhere, and he wanted to follow all the roads in the world.

He had fallen into a doze by the fire when the door of the main cabin opened and G.G. bounced in with a pair of fishing rods.

"Look!" he said. "Some guys loaned me these and the rain has stopped. Come on. We can fish from the dock. All we need is bait."

With two sharp sticks they soon dug up enough mud to find four worms, which they put into a paper cup. G.G. said that four worms would give them two spares. There were plenty more where those came from if the fish were really biting. He handed a rod to Josh and took the path to the camp dock.

"I've never fished," Josh said.

"That's O.K.," G.G. told him. "There's nothing to it. Except putting the worm on the hook is a gooky job." He unwound his fishing line and squatted down on the dock. "See, the hook goes about halfway through the worm, like this. And then the end of the worm goes on the hook once or twice, like this."

Josh baited his hook. It was a gooky job.

"You can take the end of the dock. I'll take the side," G.G. said. "Now cast your line, like this . . . Don't let your line swing around so much or someone could get hooked, me. And there you are."

With his line safely in the water, Josh asked, "How will I know if I catch a fish?"

"You'll feel a tug. If you do, let the fish play with the hook for a moment, then reel him in."

Josh had always wondered how fishing could be any fun, just standing around waiting. Now he learned why it was fun. Nothing was happening, but something might happen at any minute, and that was exciting.

Suddenly G.G. called, "Got one!" His rod was bending, he reeled in his line, and a moment later a small silvery fish was twisting and flopping on the dock.

"Now what?" asked Josh, coming to see.

"Better keep an eye on your own line," said G.G., "but here's what. You hold the fish like this, firm but not too tight, and take the hook out of its mouth, see? It got my worm." He dropped the fish back into the water. "Too small to eat."

Behind them, Crane's voice spoke reproachfully. "Poor little fish. It looked hungry and tired. I'm glad it got the worm. It deserved a break."

"Cut it out," G.G. said. "If you don't want to fish, why don't you go away?"

But Crane hung around. "Your line is too slack," she said to Josh. "You ought to reel it in a little."

"What do you know about it?" he asked defensively.

"I just know," she said.

Josh gave a few turns to his reel and the line tightened. Another turn and the rod began to bend.

"Got one!" he cried. He could tell that it was a monster from the way the rod was bending. He pulled hard. Then the line went slack again, and the hook came out of the water.

"The weight must have hit bottom," Crane said. "It probably got tangled in a weed. That would feel as if you had a fish on the hook."

Josh was impressed. "Have you done a lot of fishing?"

Crane shook her head. "Never. I just know." She looked at the dangling hook. "Poor little hopeless worm," she said.

"Listen, Crane," said G.G., "why don't you beat it? We were having fun until you came."

"I'm only trying to help," she said huffily, and settled down to stay.

Presently Josh felt a tug on his line. It was no mistake this time. He had caught a fish. He reeled it in triumphantly while Crane and G.G. came to look.

"Hold on to it," G.G. reminded him, "and work the hook out of its mouth."

Crane sniffed. "That's the same fish. I remember its face. How can you be so mean to it?"

"Mean?" Josh protested. "I didn't ask it to swim over here." The wet and slippery fish thumped and thrashed on the dock while Josh worked at the hook. Under Crane's accusing eyes, his fingers were making a mess of it.

"I'll do it," G.G. offered, and Josh was glad to let him. Once again, G.G. dropped the fish into the lake.

Crane said, "Ugh!" and took herself off.

Josh and G.G. had no more luck. They dug up extra worms and baited their hooks with the juiciest ones, but the fish were tricky. They took the bait and never touched the hooks.

"Crane spoiled the fishing," Josh said at last. "We're just feeding the fish."

But G.G. said, "Never give up." And just then Josh had a bite. A thrill went down his arms and all the way to his toes as he felt the tug and knew that he had a big fish, a game fish, a fish worth catching. He tussled with it, reeling it in, holding on, while G.G. helped and advised, until at last Josh pulled his fish onto the dock. It was a prize catch.

"A bass," G.G. said, "and big enough for dinner. Congratulations! He who waits will get!"

G.G. removed the hook, and when the big fish had stopped flopping, Josh carried it up to the main cabin. Dusty cleaned it. Muff cooked it.

"And Crane," Josh said later to G.G., "ate as much as anybody."

9 ❀ ❀

That night, from somewhere in the dark, there came a strange, crazy laugh, then silence. Then a long, shuddering howl. Josh woke and lay stiff and motionless in his sleeping bag. Neither Dusty nor G.G. moved or spoke. Josh wondered whether they were asleep or as scared as he was. Had those sounds come from an animal in the woods or from some person in one of the cabins? It sounded like the cackling of the awful woman in the movie *The Wizard of Oz* who had started out on a bicycle and had turned into a witch on a broomstick. Crane wouldn't be laughing and howling like that, would she? Several times in the night, between waking and sleeping, Josh heard the sounds again, and each time they scared him.

In the morning, Crane looked and sounded just as usual, no better, no worse. The weather had cleared, and she was excited when Dusty said that the first event of the day would be a visit to a natural-science center.

This was a great success. Muff came by truck. She joined the others when they left their bicycles and set off on foot to follow a trail through woods, glens, and hollows. A sign read PLEASE TAKE ONLY PICTURES AND LEAVE ONLY FOOTPRINTS. Along the path, animals and birds could be seen in their natural homes, and the very first exhibit cleared up last night's mystery. A rustic shelter showed maps and models of where and how loons built their nests.

"Did you hear them last night?" Crane asked Josh excitedly. "They laugh. It sounds—loony."

"I heard it," Josh said. "I thought—" But she hurried ahead too fast to hear. Josh grinned to himself. It was funny what he had thought. Now that they were getting friendlier, she might think it was funny too, but better not push his luck.

Deer were feeding on a grassy knoll. Wild geese floated on a little pond. Bobcats and raccoons made their homes in thickets along the trail. Signs explained how each was part of the wonderful plan of nature. Everyone liked the natural-science center, and Crane could not tear herself away. While they waited for her in the parking lot, G.G. said, "It would be great if Crane liked people as well as she likes animals."

"Animals never criticize," Muff said. "They take you the way you are. I think that's one reason Crane likes them. She's shy, you know."

Muff and I, A TRUCK chugged away on the next leg of the day's trip. They were going to have a picnic lunch on the top of a mountain that overlooked Big Pine Lake. Dusty said they should have leg muscles like rocks by this time, but the mountain road presented a challenge.

"This will separate the men from the boys," he predicted. "And maybe the boys from the girls, Crane. But we're not trying to prove anything. Remember to shift down when you go uphill, and try to stay at the same pace. Then you won't get so tired. And if any of us can't make it, we can always get off and push our bikes the rest of the way."

They soon saw what he meant. None of them was a match for Dusty's age, size, and strength. He easily took the lead on the mountain road and kept it. G.G. held his own in second place, and Josh followed G.G. Crouched over his handlebars, he put his back into the job of getting up the mountain, and wished for more gears on his bike. Crane was somewhere behind him. He thought about what Muff had said. Muff was usually right, and Helen too had said that Crane was shy. Some girls were smart about knowing things like that. But Crane did not seem like a shrinking violet to Josh, and he was ready to bet that she would rather die than admit defeat by pushing her bike up that mountain. She might have tender feelings. She could also be hard as nails.

Dusty had said there was no contest among themselves, but there was a grueling contest with the mountain. Josh was pitting his stamina against the relentless climb from one hairpin turn to another. Sweat soaked his body, and his eyes were glazed in an agony of concentration on the stretch of road one turn ahead of his front wheel. He kept on cranking his pedals, determined to finish well. Then he heard a cheer, and saw Muff, Dusty, and G.G. waving him on. When he swung off his bike beside them at the top of the mountain, panting and dizzy, he knew he had won another victory of the sort that only bicycling can give.

If he had had any breath left, the view from the top would have taken it away. Far below, on a green carpet of woods, little lakes shone like the splinters of a mirror broken and scattered by some mountain giant. Crane would love this. But where was she?

"I'll give her five minutes," Muff said. "Then I'll

go and get her with the truck." She poured a welcome drink of hunnigar for the three while they collapsed on the ground to relax and massage their sore muscles.

No Crane appeared. Muff got into the truck and started downhill on her rescue mission, but she returned almost immediately.

"Crane is coming," she said. "She has to stop and rest now and then, but she won't take a lift. She's determined to pedal all the way."

It seemed like a long time until Crane rounded the last bend, toiling valiantly up the final slope, her bike wobbling, her face pale with fatigue but triumphant.

"You have to hand it to her," Josh said. "She made it on her own." The Bunch cheered her until they were hoarse.

Yet that very evening they were all complaining about another typical Crane stunt. Late in the afternoon they had rented two canoes from the Big Pine Youth Hostel and had paddled to an island that looked like a pleasant goal within easy distance. As they neared the island, they saw that rocks rose like walls from the water's edge, topped by thick tangles of green, as if the island did not welcome visitors.

At last, circling along the shore, they had come to a hidden cove and beached the canoes. Then they explored separately, jumping over stones and fallen logs, scuffling through dry leaves, calling back and forth to each other. Suddenly Josh came upon Crane kneeling on a rocky ledge that lay half in shade, half in sun. She was moving some things from a shady spot to a sunny one. Thin black wiggling things. Worms? They were awfully long for worms.

"Snakes," said Crane happily, when she saw Josh. "Baby snakes. Aren't they cute? They like to be warm, so I'm helping them."

"Snakes!" Josh yelled.

"You don't know much about snakes," Crane said pityingly. "It's only in stories and movies that they're always bad."

Then it all happened very quickly. Muff, Dusty, and G.G., having heard Josh's yell, came running. Josh heard behind him a buzz, as if seeds were shaking in a gourd. He turned and saw a thing as long as a belt sliding toward him over the dead leaves. He did not need to know much about snakes to recognize this one. At his foot was a stone the size of a football. Josh lifted it and heaved it, striking the rattlesnake just behind the head.

"You killed it," Dusty said. "Good job." But though the words were cool, his voice sounded strained.

Crane looked down from her ledge, still holding a baby snake in her hand. "Oh," she said. "It was a rattler. Then these are—"

Everyone panicked. "Drop it, Crane. For Pete's sake, drop it!"

Crane dropped the snake and jumped down from the ledge.

"Where there's one rattler, there can be another," G.G. said, talking fast. "Let's get out of here."

"Move!" Dusty agreed. "One rattlesnake is enough for me."

They made for the canoes, keeping a sharp lookout underfoot for snakes.

"From now on, Crane, don't be so—so innocent," Muff warned. "If those were baby rattlers, they could have bitten you. You don't know enough about snakes to take chances. Did they have buttons on their tails?"

Crane nodded contritely.

"Then they were rattlers," Muff said. "Luckily, you have gentle hands. But remember, snakes like their privacy as much as people do."

Josh guessed how Crane would have answered at the start of this trip: "I know none of you like me." She would have turned away and sulked. And he would have thought of a witch's brew made with snakes.

Now Crane only said quite meekly, "I know I was dumb." To Josh she said, "Thanks for what you did."

He couldn't believe it. She had actually said thanks.

"Are you coming with me?" he asked. He headed

for the shore and stepped into a canoe. Then he took the seat in the bow and looked back at her as she stood hesitating on the beach.

"Can you stand it if I come?" she asked.

"I can stand it," he said.

She pushed the canoe into clear water and hopped into the stern seat, smiling.

While they crossed the lake back to the hostel, Josh taught Crane the canoe song that he had learned at Camp Buddy:

My paddle's keen and bright, flashing with silver,
Follow the wild-goose flight, dip, dip, and swing;
Dip, dip, and swing it back, flashing with silver,
Follow the wild-goose track, dip, dip, and swing.

They paddled back in perfect rhythm.

10 ❀ ❀

The Bunch were lying in a row on a little beach by a mountain stream, looking up at the night sky. It was the last leg of their trip, which was probably just as well, because the truck seemed to be on its last legs too. Its cheerful slogan, I, A TRUCK, AM DOING THE BEST I CAN, was barely visible under dust and mud. The poor old truck had a deep cough and it had the shakes. The supply of books had long since overflowed the shoe box and spilled on the floor. Dusty said he would have made a book shelf if he had known how many books they would have collected by the end of the trip. G.G. had finished *The Hobbit* and added it to the original pile. Crane had contributed a bird guide, a tree guide, and a star guide that she had bought along the way, and there were dozens of free pamphlets picked up wherever they had stopped to sight-see.

No one could be sure how many hundreds of miles the Bunch had pedaled. Josh's sleeping bag leaked feathers from several holes, and his bike, already old at the start of the trip, now badly needed to be overhauled. Muff said that the Bunch needed to be overhauled too, with hot showers, laundry, a dry place to sleep, and all they could eat.

Muff was the only one who still looked civilized. As for the rest, their socks and sneakers were in holes. Their clothes had been rained on, stepped on, slept in, and there were odd new touches. Dusty wore a long white loon feather on his fatigue hat. G.G. had lost his baseball cap and now wrapped his head every day in a towel, like a turban. Josh's cowboy hat was the best thing he had, and he thought gratefully of Amos Walker every time he put it on. Crane had looked like a mess all along, so she was not much different now, but she had got bored with her Band-Aid and her nose had peeled painfully.

"I don't care how I look. I want to live like this forever and ever," she sighed. "I'll never be really free again, not unless I take another trip, and no trip could ever be quite the same as this one." The others were silent, knowing that it was true.

Often now, they lay awake at night, looking up at the stars and talking companionably instead of going to sleep at once as they had done when the trip began. Tonight Dusty talked about having a place of his own someday. He had lived in an orphanage, and at Camp Buddy, and in Marine Corps barracks, and he did not want to live like that much longer. He had his house all planned, a house on an island, where time did not matter, where there were no schedules.

Crane said she wanted to live in a tent. G.G. said he could never live anywhere but New York. Josh was silent. Right now all he wanted was to keep traveling forever.

"I've been thinking," Muff said. "I'm going to keep working on the farm until I have enough money to buy a little bus. Then I'm going to fill it with books and drive around the country where people want something to read. I'll have a book exchange. I'll sell some, but most I'll just give away. I wouldn't have thought of it if I hadn't come on this trip."

They listened for a while to the wilderness quiet and the lively sound of water talking to itself as it flowed around rocks and hurried over shallows. Farther downstream there was roaring white water. While they had cooked their supper, occasional bold adventurers, with rafts or canoes, had passed along the river on their way to challenge that wild passage.

"I'm going to canoe on white water," Josh said, "someday, before I get old."

"I'm already getting old," Crane said. "I'm going to be thirteen tomorrow."

They all mumbled congratulations and fell silent, wondering how they could celebrate Crane's birthday. There was no way to buy real presents or have a real party. The nearest town was miles away. Tomorrow they could do no more than take a last swim in the river, and eat their last meals together, simple, campfire meals. Then they would take their last ride, a short one back to Gitche Gumee Campground. They would have come full circle to their starting point. Josh and G.G. would go in the truck to Rivertown, where they would board trains for home. Crane's brother Alan would meet her at the campground with a car to drive her home. Muff would go back to the farm, and Dusty was off to his new Marine center.

But first there would be Crane's birthday. Josh wished that he could give her a present—and he could have, now that he had got his wallet and money back—but where would he buy one?

In the morning, Josh found Muff, Dusty, and G.G. poking around among the last of the food supplies in the truck.

"Here's some cake mix that we never used," Muff said doubtfully. "And here's an egg. That's all you need except water. If we could make a birthday cake—"

"We haven't got an oven," G.G. pointed out.

"I might make one," Dusty offered. "But don't tell Crane what I'm doing in case it doesn't work. Muff, you take her up the river for a swim after breakfast. The rest of us will get the party ready, somehow or other."

He built a fire between two logs, and laid the grill on the logs. It was a good fire for cooking. While the others drank the last of the canned juice, G.G. fried the last of the bacon. It was the last time for everything.

"This is the last time I'll be the cook," G.G. said. "I never thought I'd miss it, but I will."

"It's my turn for K.P.," Crane said, "but I won't miss that."

"I'll do it for you," Josh said. "Call it a birthday present."

After breakfast, Muff and Crane went off for their swim. Josh scoured the skillet with river sand and helped to tackle the making of Crane's birthday cake. Dusty built up the fire to make long-lasting embers and told G.G. to hunt for flat stones. Then all three constructed a stone oven over the fire. They calked the holes between the stones with mud and gravel, leaving one side of the oven open. G.G. mixed the cake batter and poured it into a pan. A final stone closed the hole. They stood back, hands on hips, and admired their oven.

"Will it work?" Josh wondered aloud.

"That's what we're going to find out," said Dusty.

An hour later they carefully opened the oven. Inside was a cake, a real cake.

"At least it looks like a cake," G.G. said, "but it needs some icing. What have we got for icing?"

Josh went to hunt among the supplies in the truck. "There's brown sugar," he called. "That's about all." Then he looked at the box more carefully. "To make caramel icing," he read. "Brown sugar, milk, margarine . . . Hey! We can make it, and caramel is Crane's favorite!"

They found enough milk and margarine. "But who's going to make the icing?" Dusty asked. "It might be tricky."

"Let's count out," Josh said. He grinned and began to point his finger. "Intery, mintery, cutery, corn—" It was Crane's counting-out rhyme, and it ended with his finger pointing at himself. He, Josh, who had never cooked, who had done extra K.P. on the entire trip to avoid cooking, was now elected by fate to add the final touch to Crane's birthday cake.

The hot oven could not be touched, so Dusty built a second fire between logs and Josh went to work on the icing. Mixing it was no problem. The cooking was the tricky part. G.G. and Dusty were full of helpful advice.

"Don't let it burn . . . No, it has to boil some more . . . Double, double, toil and trouble . . . More yet . . . More yet . . . Now!"

There is a magic moment when a sticky icing mix turns into icing. Josh poured, smoothed, and swirled his mixture just in time before the icing hardened.

"A masterpiece!" Dusty proclaimed it. "A chef couldn't do better!"

"Write something on it," G.G. suggested.

So Josh wrote with a knife on the icing, HAPPY BIRTHDAY CRANE.

There was only time to hide the cake in the truck and to open some cans of spaghetti and meatballs before the girls came back from their swim.

Dusty filled the plates and mixed up a last batch of hunnigar. "This is just the first course," he said.

Crane exclaimed over the spaghetti and meatballs as if it had been a gourmet dish of her own making. "What did you put in it? It's delicious!"

"It's right out of the can," Josh said. "We should have added some mushrooms."

But Crane was in no mood to criticize the canned

spaghetti and meatballs. She helped to polish off the first course like a young wolf.

Then Josh produced the cake and set it in front of her. She covered her face with her hands. "Oh!" she said. "Oh!"

Dusty took out his harmonica and gave them the key for "Happy Birthday." They had sung it all the way through before Crane uncovered her face, and Josh saw that at that moment Crane was beautiful, as beautiful as Helen.

"I made the icing," he said. "It's caramel."

They ate up the last crumb of the cake with the last of the hunnigar.

There were even some presents for Crane's birthday. G.G. retrieved his copy of *The Hobbit* from the truck library and gave it to her. Dusty was presenting her with his loon feather, when a raft came floating down the river with three travelers aboard. What's cooking?" they called.

The Bunch shouted, "Crane's birthday!" pointing at her.

"Happy birthday to you, happy birthday to you!" The three travelers waved and sang. Then they were gone, on their way to white water. "Happy birthday, dear Crane . . ." Their voices faded.

Crane was crying. "I can't help it," she said. "I don't want to be a drip, but everyone is so nice to me."

And even crying, she was beautiful. "What can I give you?" She thought a moment. Then she unpinned her veil and pulled it from her hat. "Muff, take my veil, will you? And G.G., you can have my cat pin. Dusty, here's my recorder. Maybe you can learn 'The Keys to Canterbury.' You already know most of it. And Josh—" She picked up a round, smooth stone. "This is for you. It's caramel color, see?"

After the party, Crane had one last crazy idea. She thought of a way to make a sauna out of the stone oven.

"We can park the bicycles around the oven and cover them with ponchos. That will make a tent. Then we pour water over the hot stones and sit in the steam until we cook. And *then* we jump in the river!"

Everyone thought it was worth a try, and after they tried it, they agreed that they felt like a million dollars.

"Even if we're broke," Dusty said.

"I'm not broke," Josh pointed out. "Since I got my wallet back, I'm loaded. Anyone who needs dough, just ask me." As it turned out, no one needed dough. Sharing expenses, bicycling, and camping, they had not spent much.

For the last time, they doused their campfire and packed their bikes. Amid fluttering feathers, Josh rolled up his sleeping bag and strapped it to his luggage carrier. It was time to start. But when the caravan was ready, I, A TRUCK would not start.

"Poor old truck," Muff said. "The battery's dead or something. You all go ahead and send a repair truck from the first filling station you see. I can take care of myself—and goodbye, in case I don't see you again." Her voice was unsteady. "There's no use dragging out the goodbyes."

They were all stunned. Say goodbye to Muff just like that? Just goodbye and go? They couldn't.

"I'm not saying goodbye," Dusty told her. And then, as if surprised by his own words, "You can't take care of yourself this time, Muff. At least, I won't let you. The rest of you go on and wait for us at Gitche Gumee. I'm staying with Muff until I get this truck started, if it's the last thing I do." Dusty was looking at Muff the way she had been looking at him all along. It was clear to Josh that Dusty thought Muff was beautiful. Probably he didn't even see the scar on her chin any more. Come to think of it, Josh himself hadn't noticed it since the very first day, not since the moment when he had seen Muff's smile. Well, thought Josh, it had taken Dusty a while to get interested, but he certainly had a super girl.

So it was that the three younger bicyclists pedaled off by themselves and came to the last hill on the road to Gitche Gumee Campground. G.G. was in the lead,

106

followed by Crane, and Josh was bringing up the rear when it occurred to him that if Crane's brother Alan, head prefect at Oakley School, was going to see them arrive, he, Joshua Cobb, was going to be the first in line.

He gave a fast turn to his pedals, passed Crane, and then applied his foot brake for safety. No brake. Josh squeezed his hand brake. Zilch! His bike only gathered speed. Followed by a drift of feathers from his tattered sleeping bag, he came bucketing down the hill, past G.G. Suddenly he hit fresh tar. It spattered up from his front wheel and settled on him. Ahead he saw the GITCHE GUMEE CAMPGROUND sign. Tarred and feathered, he whizzed into the dirt road through the grounds, narrowly missing a station wagon parked near the entrance.

It was only when he had bumped and jolted to a stop that he saw who was in the station wagon. Alan Crane was at the wheel, and beside him sat Helen. She waved to Josh and smiled. Then she called in the low, clear voice that was not like any other voice, "Josh! Hi, there! What a finish!"

Josh knew that he looked like a mess. But Helen sounded as if he looked all right, as if he had just won a race, or a battle. She always made him feel great.

Before he could answer, Crane and G.G. arrived and they were all talking at once. They were still

107

jabbering away, trying to tell Alan Crane everything that had happened on the trip, when they heard a familiar cough behind them, and there was I, A TRUCK, with Dusty and Muff together in the cab, looking very happy. The Bunch had finished the trip. They had all arrived safely at their journey's end.

"I don't see how you did it," Helen said, "but I wish I could have done it too."

"It was easy," Crane told her. "I took care of everybody. At least, I tried to. You said I should. I guess we all took care of each other. Every day was magic."

Josh and G.G. put their bikes into the truck and climbed in after them. Alan was putting Crane's bike into the station wagon when Muff started the engine and I, A TRUCK began to shudder with effort. Now it was really time to say goodbye. As Muff had put it, there was no point in dragging out the goodbyes. That would make them feel worse. But no one wanted to say it.

Crane and Helen went together to say it to Dusty and Muff. "You're going to keep on taking care of each other," Crane told them, as if she were seeing it in a crystal ball. Then she came with Helen to the rear of the truck and stood there looking up. You could tell they were sisters, Josh thought. Both of them were beautiful.

"Remember, you promised me the first dance in the fall," he said to Helen.

He was just wondering what to say to Crane when she held out her arms as if she wanted to hug the truck and cried, "Don't ever forget me! Always be my friends!"

"Always," Josh said.

And Helen said to G.G., "I wish I could see more of you, too."

And G.G. made his last joke. "You can't see any more of me. This is all there is."

And I, A TRUCK chugged away.